AN ENCORE FOR ESTELLE

MELODIES OF LOVE
BOOK TWO

KIMBERLY ROSE JOHNSON

An Encore for Estelle
Published by Sweet Rose Press
U.S.A.

This is a work of fiction. Names, characters, places and incidents are either the product of the author's imagination or are used fictitiously, and any resemblance to actual persons, living or dead, business establishments, events or locales is entirely coincidental.

All Scripture quotations, unless otherwise indicated, are taken from the Holy Bible, New International Version®, NIV®. Copyright ©1973, 1978, 1984, 2011 by Biblica, Inc.™ Used by permission of Zondervan. All rights reserved worldwide. www.zondervan.com The "NIV" and "New International Version" are trademarks registered in the United States Patent and Trademark Office by Biblica, Inc.™

Acknowledgements

As with most any book it takes a village to get it ready for publication. I would like to thank my team: critique partners, Margaret Daley, Vickie McDonough, Miralee Ferrell; copy editor, Jenny Mertes; formatter, Cindy Jackson; beta readers, Preslaysa Williams, Becky G. Smith and Janice Sisemore; and proofreaders, Edward Arrington, Marylin Farumasu, Becky Dempsey, and Beverley Lytle.

Finally I would like to extend a huge thank you to Angela Ruth Strong. You challenged me to take this book to a different level with your thorough critique. I can't thank you enough for all the hard work you put into this book. You rock!

1

Estelle Rogers willed her galloping heart to slow. Why had she come back to Oak Knoll, Oregon? It wasn't like the people here had welcomed her with open arms six years ago. But that was then. Things were different now. Helen Wood had invited her for a visit over the summer, and she could never say no to the one woman who'd accepted her in spite of her flaws. Besides, she needed time away to think about her future. Estelle squared her shoulders, raised a hand, and pressed the doorbell beside the farmhouse door.

The door flung open. "You're here!" Helen's smile lit her eyes.

Estelle blinked. Helen looked like a young Mary Tyler Moore—she looked fantastic. Could this be the same woman she'd grown close to all those years ago? Granted when she'd last seen Helen, she'd been recovering from a stroke, but a different woman stood before her now. The rosy-cheeked brunette looked fifteen years younger than her fifty-five years. "You look amazing."

Helen blushed and waved a hand in front of her face. "Derek sent me on a spa vacation. You should try one. You'd love it."

The mention of her one-time boyfriend didn't affect her like it used to. Helen's son was now happily married, and she adored his wife, Kayla. "If I didn't know better, I'd say you're hinting that I need a makeover."

The older woman shrugged. "Not at all. You look lovely as usual." She stepped back, opening the door wider. "Come in. I can't believe you're actually here. I was afraid you might change your mind."

"How silly would I be to do something like that?" If Helen only knew how many times she had almost cancelled the trip. But she would never reveal that to her dear friend.

Helen looped her arm through Estelle's. "I prepared lunch for us in the garden."

"I love your garden. It's so serene. I'm glad the weather is cooperating today. I noticed you've had a lot of rain lately."

"We have, but summer doesn't usually start here until July. Welcome back to Oregon." She chuckled. "I remember how much you enjoyed my garden the last time you were here, so I've been praying the weather would cooperate."

Of course she had. Helen was like that—she had no qualms about asking the Lord for a sunny day.

"You'll be staying in the guest cottage while you're

here."

Estelle stilled. "I thought your . . ." What does one call a man who works around the farm doing odd jobs? "handyman—"

"His name is Blake, and he moved into the barn so you could have the cottage."

"That was nice of him, but the barn?"

Helen patted her arm. "Now don't you worry about Blake. He's a grown man and can take care of himself. Besides, he and Derek built a nice room out there. He has all the comforts of home."

Estelle raised a brow. "If you say so."

"I do." She guided them through the house and out the French doors that led to the courtyard garden.

Estelle caught her breath. Water bubbled from a fountain near the cottage. A light breeze rustled the leaves on the birch trees overhead. A large vase of multi-colored flowers sat in the center of a round table covered with a white cloth. "It's more beautiful than I remember. You've added some new features."

"I'm glad you like it. This space has been a labor of love. I spend as much time as I am able to out here." She motioned toward a wooden chair padded with pillows. "Have a seat. I'm so pleased you finally took me up on my offer to take an extended vacation."

"Me too. Although whether I stay the entire three months you had in mind is up in the air. If I'm needed in LA, I'll have to return." There was no way she could put Jeff off for three months—it wouldn't be fair to either of them.

"Of course. After all, you're a woman in constant demand. What with your restaurant and acting career."

"I don't know how in demand I am these days. I gave up acting years ago, and my restaurant runs smoothly thanks to my executive chef and my fantastic manager. Between those two, the only thing I'm needed for is paying the bills." She sat up taller. "What's for lunch?" She wasn't hungry, but anything was better than talking about her professional life.

Helen's face lit up as she pulled the cloth off a serving tray. "I prepared a chicken salad, fresh fruit, and for dessert I made homemade peach ice cream."

"That sounds delicious." She allowed Helen to serve her then bowed her head as her hostess offered a blessing for the food.

"Amen." Helen placed a cloth napkin in her lap. "I wasn't sure what you like, but I remembered you enjoyed this dish when you were last here."

"You have a good memory, especially considering you'd had a stroke shortly before I arrived. I'm surprised you remember much about those weeks."

"I recall pretty much everything. It wasn't like I had a lot to do to fill my mind. Having you here helped with my therapy."

How had she not managed to find the time to visit this sweet woman sooner, and more important why had she been so nervous? Helen was as kind and genuine in person as she'd been in their weekly correspondence these past six years.

Helen's face brightened as she looked past Estelle. "Good afternoon, Blake. I'd like you to meet a friend. She's the one staying in the cottage."

Estelle turned to face the man. She sucked in a breath. He had to be over six feet tall. His dark hair had a messy look that she liked. *Get it together.* He wasn't the first ruggedly handsome man she'd ever met. Plus there was Jeff.

He looked down at her with chocolate brown eyes. "It's nice to meet you. Helen has told me all about you."

Estelle shot a look toward Helen. "Don't believe everything you hear."

"Believe every word, Blake." Helen waved a finger toward Estelle. "My friend here is a remarkable woman."

Estelle's face warmed. There was nothing remarkable about her, but people had always said stuff like that about her. Although it had never bothered her before, it did coming from Helen. She thought Helen knew her well enough to know she wasn't all that.

Blake grinned, although it looked forced. "I'm heading to town. Did either of you need me to get anything while I'm there?"

"No thanks, but maybe Estelle would like to join you." She raised a brow toward her.

Estelle caught her breath. Was her hostess trying to play matchmaker? She ought to warn her to give up now, because she was a relationship disaster. At least that's what she felt like.

"How about it?" Blake asked. "Would you like to come along?" His words were friendly enough, but the look in his eyes was guarded. Almost like the last thing he wanted was for her to say yes.

Why did he seem wary? She didn't recall ever meeting him—she would have remembered. "No thanks. I should finish my lunch then get settled."

He dipped his head. "Okay then. See you around." He turned and headed in the direction from which he'd come.

Estelle sat back into the chair she'd vacated when Blake showed up.

Helen leaned forward and lowered her voice. "Isn't he cute?"

She burst into laughter. "You are old enough to be his mother."

"I didn't say I wanted to marry him. Goodness." She frowned.

Estelle sobered. "I'm sorry, Helen. I didn't mean to offend you."

"Sorry, I overreacted. I'm fine. Don't give it another thought." She fanned her flushed face. "One would think at my age that I'd stop blushing so easily, but it appears that trait will forever plague me."

"At least when you blush you're pretty. When I blush, my neck turns red, and I get all blotchy." Estelle made a silly face. "It happened once on set, and the director was not happy. They had to take time out for the makeup artist to cover the red before we could

6

continue filming."

Helen bubbled with laughter. "It's going to be fun having you here. Have you given any thought to how you'll fill your time? I know three months is a long vacation."

"I agree, and like I said, I may not stay the entire time. I have no idea how I'll fill my days." It'd been forever since she'd had the freedom to do whatever she wanted. There always seemed to be something or someone that needed her attention.

"You could volunteer at the community center. Every summer they do a children's theater program. Auditions are coming up, and they'll begin rehearsals soon." She dipped her head and fiddled with her fork.

"You know I don't act anymore."

"So you said, but those kids don't care. They'd be thrilled to have a real actress—" she raised a hand, "former actress mentor them. A little birdie told me you used to volunteer with the children's theater in LA."

Estelle sighed. It had been a long time since she'd done anything with the children's theater. She liked kids, but she'd left that life. Then again, this was Helen asking. "I'll think about it."

"Don't think too long. My son tells me this new musical is ambitious for such a small town, and Blake needs help."

If Derek was concerned then there was probably reason to be. "What does Blake have to do with the children's theater?"

"Didn't I mention that it's his brainchild? He coordinates the program. I'm hoping you'll stick around through the summer and help him. The theater has become a big deal here, and no matter what Blake thinks, he can't keep doing it all on his own."

Estelle shook her head. This must be the real reason for Helen's invitation to spend the summer with her. Not that she minded, but wished her friend had been upfront about the reason behind her request. "You neglected to mention any of this." She felt snookered, but it was fine. She'd do almost anything for Helen. Plus the timing worked—at least for now. If she could manage to stay away from her restaurant and her life for three months remained to be seen. If necessary she could fly home a couple of times to check up on things. The idea of working with the theater sent a tingle of excitement zipping through her. That settled it—she was in if Blake would have her. She loved the theater.

"What's that little smile about?" Helen asked.

"I have no idea." Estelle plopped a raspberry into her mouth.

They finished their lunch in companionable silence. Estelle couldn't stop thinking about the children's theater. She had so many questions but would save them for Blake.

~

Blake Price lifted the tailgate to his Ford pickup then

made his way inside the community center. The sound of skidding athletic shoes met his ears as soon as he stepped inside. He breathed easy for the first time since being introduced to Estelle. He couldn't help smiling. There was something about this place that made everything feel okay again.

"Hi, Blake." The thirteen-year-old dark-haired girl who looked too much like his daughter ambled toward him. "My mom said I can try out for the musical."

He stilled and forced a smile. "That's great, Jenny. Auditions are on Friday. Do you have what you need?" He liked Jenny, but she reminded him of Kendal. A weight settled on him. It would be difficult to have Jenny in the musical as a constant reminder of his failure as a husband and dad, but if she was half as good a singer as he'd been told, he'd be out of his mind to not give her a part that featured her voice.

"I think I have everything." She slid her backpack off and pulled out the score. Everyone who auditioned would be singing the same song.

"Perfect. See you Friday." He patted her shoulder and moved toward the door that led backstage.

He'd been writing and producing a musical every summer for the past three years. This year's musical would be the biggest yet, especially since Derek Wood had written such a stellar score. Blake smiled, thinking of the dialogue he'd written. The collaboration had been fun, but now the real work started—casting, his least favorite part of producing, and directing. He hated disappointing the kids, because inevitably some of them wouldn't get the role they wanted. With this year's musical being longer and more complex, he hoped they could pull it off as well as they had done in previous years.

"There you are," a vaguely familiar female voice said.

He turned. "Estelle." His pulse accelerated. The blonde beauty was anything but beautiful on the inside, and he wanted nothing to do with her. "What are you doing here?" He winced at the accusatory tone to his voice. "Sorry. I didn't mean—"

She waved a hand. "It's fine. I can tell I startled you."

He closed his eyes for a brief second, willing his pulse to slow. "What can I do for you?"

"As you know, I'm spending an extended period of time in Oak Knoll per Helen's request. It didn't take long for me to realize I'll go stir crazy if I don't find some way to occupy my time. I heard about your little musical, and I was hoping you'd let me help in some way."

Little musical? He clamped his teeth together. "I don't know. I'm kind of a control freak."

She pursed her pretty lips together. He took in her delicate features and stunning blue eyes. He shook his head. He could not think about her pretty lips or any other part of her. Estelle was off limits as far as he was concerned.

"I've worked with control freaks before, and we all

survived." She chuckled. "You should meet my executive chef. Now that man is a control freak." She shot him a heart-melting smile.

He stopped himself from groaning just in time. He could not give in to her simply because she was beautiful.

"Please, Blake. You'd be doing me a huge favor. I needed to get away from home for a while, and sitting around doing nothing will give me too much time to think." Sincerity filled her eyes. "As it happens I have some theater experience."

Confusion filled him. Could he have been misinformed about the true nature of this woman? He thrust the thought aside for now. "I assumed you only did movies." He winced. Acknowledging he knew her credits and still rejected her help had to be insulting to Estelle. After all, there was a time when any director in Hollywood would have killed to have her in their movie—but no more. From what he'd heard, her last movie role had been a flop. His late wife, Trinity's dancing eyes flitted through his mind. She'd met Estelle once while working on a movie set and had said Estelle Rogers had been rude to her. That alone would keep him away from the woman.

Regardless, Trinity would be excited that a movie star offered to work with him on something he wrote, even if it was a star she didn't care for. She'd supported his writing one hundred percent. If only he hadn't failed her when she needed him the most, she'd still be here— along with their daughter. His heart constricted.

"I did do movies. I don't anymore." Estelle rested a hand on his arm. Concern covered her face. "Are you all right?"

He shifted, causing her to remove her hand. "Sorry. I went to another time and place for a moment. Let me think about your offer, and I'll get back to you."

"That sounds fair. So you know, I can sew, cook, organize volunteers, help with the set . . ." She rested a hand on her hip. "I'm wasting my breath, aren't I?"

"Not at all. It's good to know your various talents." A sudden thought hit him. Estelle might be an answer to prayer now that he thought about it. "I actually have the perfect job for you, and you'd be saving me a lot of angst."

Her face lit. "Shoot."

"Auditions are on Friday. I'd appreciate a second pair of ears and eyes."

"I thought you were a control freak?"

"I am." He sighed. "Okay, I'm only saying this once, so listen." He looked around and lowered his voice. "I dread auditions. They are the hardest part of this whole thing for me."

"Seriously? Why?"

"They just are. Can you help me or not?"

She nodded. Her shiny hair bounced around her heart-shaped face. "I'd be honored."

"Thanks. Auditions begin at nine sharp. Be here no later than eight."

She saluted him, clapped her heels together and then

spun around.

Was that a giggle? He watched her drift onto the stage. She glanced his way before trotting down the stairs. He shook his head. Estelle Rogers was nothing like he'd expected based on Trinity's description or even Derek's for that matter. The tabloids appeared to have been wrong about her too. As he recalled, they'd painted the picture of a diva with no heart.

Unless he'd read her wrong, she had plenty of heart. The woman he'd met was no diva, unless she was a better actress than he realized. He recalled reading somewhere that directors refused to work with her because her acting had become amateurish. That wouldn't be a problem here, unless she behaved like a child—he'd have more than enough of those to direct. The back of his neck prickled. Who was the real Estelle Rogers? The woman the media painted or the one he'd met today?

"There you are." An overly sweet female voice drew him from his musings.

He turned and sighed. "Mrs. Smith. What can I do for you?" Another thing he didn't enjoy about the theater—stage moms. Mrs. Smith was the most difficult. Because she made huge contributions to the theater every year, he couldn't afford to offend her. Without her money they wouldn't have half of the props they'd need. Too bad her daughter's acting skills were lacking.

"You can give my Melody the starring role. She's ready." The woman tried to smile, but it came across as sinister in the dim lighting.

"Auditions are on Friday. Parts will be posted by Monday of next week."

She huffed. "You owe my daughter."

He crossed his arms, and narrowed his eyes. Last season he'd found a role for *every* kid that auditioned, so this attitude made no sense. "Why is that?"

"You gave her two lines last summer. She took acting lessons this past year. She's going to be a freshman in high school in September, and it's her time to shine." A coy look crossed her face. "I haven't made my annual contribution to the theater this year. After her bit part last year, I thought I should hold off."

"Everyone receives the same chance as the others."

She crossed her arms, matching his stance. "Is that why Paris had the starring role for the past two years?" She raised a brow. "Doesn't sound fair to me."

"If the part fits her best, then it benefits everyone to have her in the lead role because she makes them and our benefactors look good." He needed her money, but he couldn't be bought. He hoped Melody's skills had improved.

"I see. So what you're saying is that Paris is a shoo-in." She harrumphed. "You create all the musicals for the children's theater. Are you sure you're not writing the role for Paris specifically?"

He raised his chin. "Mrs. Smith, I assure you that is not how I operate." How could he appease this woman without compromising his integrity? *Estelle.* "You might be pleased to know that Estelle Rogers will be helping to cast the parts this year."

The woman's face lit up. "Well, that *does* make a difference. I've said for years this place needed more than one man deciding the fate of our children." She pivoted and marched away.

"Good riddance," he mumbled. Talk about being overly dramatic. The fate of the children? Right—as if his little theater had that much power.

A chuckle from stage right drew his attention. He narrowed his eyes. "I thought you left."

Estelle stepped further into the light.

2

Poor Blake had his hands full. She felt sorry for him, but not too sorry. After all, he was a grown man. He ought to be able to handle an obnoxious stage mom or two. "I was on my way out when I remembered I need a copy of the script. I'd like to read through it before the auditions on Friday. I see now why you want my help with casting." She nodded in the direction the woman had left. "Are there more moms like that one?"

He winced. "A couple, but she's the worst. Come on, I'll get you the script."

She followed him to a nearby door. He pulled it open and yanked on an overhead chain. A lone bulb lit the tiny, drab space. "Someone must not like you," she joked.

He pawed through papers strewn over his desk. "Why do you say that?"

"I was kidding, but in all seriousness, look at this place." A worn metal desk rested against the wall with a tall file cabinet beside it. The black desk chair was the nicest thing in the compact room. "The dressing room in my first movie when I played a supporting role was bigger than this."

"Yeah, well, this isn't Hollywood. We make do with what we have to work with. It was either this or nothing." He pulled a manila envelope from under a pile. "I was going to give this to Derek so he'd have an official copy, but never got around to it."

Her heart warmed at the name. Though an ex-boyfriend, Derek was one of the kindest men she'd ever known. She was fortunate to call him a friend, especially after everything she'd put him through. "Where is Derek? I thought he and Kayla lived in town now."

"They do. I'm sure you'll run into them sooner or later. Kayla is no longer working at the florist shop though. She sold her half of the business to her business partner."

"How did I not know that? Guess I've been busier than I realized." She'd looked forward to reconnecting with Kayla, and she wanted to see her friends' daughters. She had pictures of their adorable munchkins but had never met their youngest. Mae was already two and Betsy was four. Where did the time go? She tucked the envelope into her bag. "I guess I'll see you Friday."

"For sure, but we'll probably run into one another before then, considering we are staying on the same property. By the way, how is the cottage? Did it meet your expectations?"

"It's lovely. Thanks for giving it up for me. I didn't

expect that."

"Sure thing." He dipped his chin.

If she stood there any longer things would get awkward, but for some reason she couldn't explain, being in this theater felt right, and she didn't want to leave.

Blake cleared his throat.

"I'd better go. Bye." She turned and rushed toward the door with the exit sign above it and pushed through. Bright sunshine nearly blinded her. She squinted and shielded her eyes with her hand. A dumpster rested beside the door. A gray cat slunk past. She shivered. "This place gives me the creeps." She darted toward the sidewalk about one hundred feet away.

Feet firmly planted on the sidewalk now, she took a deep breath and let it out slowly. Now what? A sign up the street for a place called Java World grabbed her attention. "Perfect." She'd get an iced green tea then head back to Helen's garden and spend the next hour or so reading through the script.

"Estelle? Estelle Rogers, is that you?"

She plastered on a smile before turning to face the female voice. Her eyes widened in recognition. "I know you. You're Kayla's business partner. I mean were. I heard you bought her out."

The woman smiled. "Good memory. And yes, I did. She wanted to be a full-time mom and be free to travel with Derek when he tours." She held out her hand. "I'm Jill."

"Of course." She winced when she thought about the way she'd acted that summer. "I owe you an apology. I wasn't very nice to you when I was last here, and I'm sorry."

Jill's mouth opened slightly. "That was unexpected."

Estelle chuckled. "I imagine so. I'm not the same person I was six years ago, and I'm embarrassed for the way I behaved the last time I was here."

"As I recall you were under a lot of stress. All is forgiven."

Pleasure poured over her like a healing balm. "Thanks. That's nice of you." Maybe she should have come back to this small town sooner. For years she'd carried the guilt of her behavior.

Jill tipped her head to the side. "What are you doing in Oak Knoll?"

"Helen asked me to visit for a few months. She's been inviting me here for years, but this is the first time my schedule has allowed it." And she was finally brave enough to face the people she'd been so rude to on her last visit.

"Wow. I didn't realize the two of you kept in touch. Kayla never said anything."

Estelle shrugged. "Helen made a huge impact on my life, and we became great friends. My only regret is not visiting sooner. This place looks exactly the way I remember."

"For the most part." Jill looked past her. "It was great seeing you. I hope you have a nice visit." She headed in the opposite direction Estelle was going.

Feeling lighter, Estelle ambled along the main drag until she reached Java World then pushed inside. She breathed in deeply the rich scent of coffee. As much as she loved the scent, she much preferred tea. Hopefully they carried it too.

"Welcome to Java World." A dark-haired woman who looked to be in her early thirties greeted her from behind the counter. Her eyes suddenly widened. "You're Estelle Rogers!" Awe lit her voice. "What are you doing here?"

Estelle inwardly cringed. In LA she was old news, but apparently in small town Oregon a former celebrity was still a big deal. "I'm visiting a friend."

"Oh." Her eyes grew even wider. "You and DJ Parker were an item." She shook her head. "I mean Derek. I was here the day you showed up and put the town in an uproar." She frowned. "That's not going to happen this time, is it?"

"I sure hope not." Estelle shifted and glanced toward the exit. Thankfully the paparazzi had no reason to follow her now—they'd always made her nervous.

"Good. Although it was great for business, I prefer our town as is." She held out her hand. "I'm Gabby."

Estelle shook it, not quite sure how to take this outspoken woman. "It's nice to meet you, Gabby."

"You too. I'm sorry for being nosy. Your life is none of my business. What can I get you?"

Estelle ordered her drink to go then waited at the

other end of the counter, thankful Gabby's questions had ceased. The shop was deserted, but the attention still felt uncomfortable. She preferred to be treated like everyone else—except when she wanted tickets to a sold-out show or concert. Then she'd milk her former celebrity status for all she could. Lately it didn't go far.

"Here's your tea. I hope you come in again."

Estelle took the iced beverage. "Thanks. I'm sure we'll be seeing a lot of each other this summer." Things were shaping up better than she'd expected.

"I'm glad." Gabby offered a sincere smile.

She headed outside into the sunshine. Her cell phone vibrated, and she pulled it out of her pocket and frowned. *Jeff.* Her thumb hovered over the screen. She told him she needed time, but maybe he was checking to make sure she arrived safely. "Hi," she said softly.

"Hi yourself. Are you there?"

"I am."

"How was the drive?"

"Long."

"I imagine it was. So . . ." He drew out the word.

"I don't have an answer yet, Jeff."

"Why? Forget it. I asked you to marry me a week ago. That is more than enough time to decide. Clearly you don't feel the way I do."

"Jeff, please don't be like this."

Silence.

Regret for hurting him filled her. "Hello?" She looked at the screen and realized he'd disconnected the call. Did she just get dumped? She huffed a breath and pocketed her phone.

This was exactly why she'd needed to get away—to clear her head and figure out what she wanted. Marriage was a huge commitment, and she needed to know for sure he was the one. But if he was willing to give up on her so easily, then he couldn't possibly be the one. Or could he?

Someone brushed past her, causing her to realize she was standing in the middle of the sidewalk not moving. *Great.* Hopefully no one noticed. She marched directly to her car, parked a block away. She tossed her bag onto the passenger seat and caught the envelope holding the script before it slipped out and fell to the floor. At least now she could totally focus on the musical's script since she didn't have to figure out whether to accept Jeff's marriage proposal.

She pushed the speed limit a little, and soon Helen's farm came into view. Peace settled over her in spite of her breakup. In fact, she felt free. There was definitely something about this place that made everything feel right again. She parked, and noting no sign of Helen, she headed straight for the cottage. Bees buzzed around flowers in the window box attached to the cottage. She breathed in the sweet scent of the purple and fuchsia flowers then walked inside. She cracked the window, allowing the scent to come in.

Now to see what kind of musical Blake had written. She half-dreaded reading it. What if it was terrible? What if everyone hated it and word got back to Hollywood that she was a part of yet another flop? She shook away the thought. No one in Hollywood cared about her anymore. But she still didn't want to be associated with garbage. She hoped and prayed this script was good.

She pulled it from her bag then sat in a comfy rocker beside the open window. An hour later she placed the final page on the floor beside her. Blake was too good to be writing for a small children's theater.

A soft knock sounded on her door.

"Come in."

Helen poked her head inside. "Will you be joining me for dinner?"

Estelle sighed. "I forgot to stop for groceries. Do you mind this once?"

"Not at all. I invited Blake too, since he doesn't have a kitchen in the barn."

"You mean he won't be able to feed himself as long as I'm here?"

"There's a mini fridge and a microwave."

"I feel like I'm putting everyone out." She pushed up out of the chair and strolled toward Helen. "First thing tomorrow, I'll look for a place to rent short term."

"Nonsense. You're my guest."

"But what about Blake?"

"He's fine." She smiled as though she hadn't a care in the world. "He knows how to feed himself. I promise you he won't starve. Even if he only has a microwave to cook with."

"Okay." How could Helen be so laissez-faire about this? *Maybe, I'm over reacting.* Being in the restaurant business probably clouded her judgment.

Her phone chimed. Everyone knew she was on vacation, and other than Jeff, her social life left a lot to be desired, so who could be texting her? Maybe Jeff had changed his mind. She dug her phone from her purse. Derek?

"I heard you're helping Blake. Let me know if you need anything. Kayla says hi."

She re-read the message three times before replying. "News travels fast. Will do. Say hi back for me. I want to see those girls of yours."

Her phone chimed again. "You're welcome any time. Mom has my address. I mean it, if you need help let me know."

"Okay." Concern nipped at the back of her mind. Why was Derek so worried about the musical? It wasn't like him to reach out like that.

~

Blake hesitated at the street corner. A line of kids and their parents trailed the length of the community center. Had the town suddenly grown more children? More than likely, many of them were from the surrounding communities. He ran a hand along his neck.

Heels clipped. He looked over his shoulder and relief washed over him. He wasn't in this alone.

Estelle wore a short red dress, denim jacket, and boots. Dark sunglasses shielded her eyes from the bright light filtering through the clouds. Her look screamed movie star. He gulped. What had he gotten himself into?

"Good morning." She stopped beside him and thrust a paper coffee cup from Java World toward him. "I didn't know what you like but took a chance on a mocha."

He raised it to his lips. Mmm—it tasted as good as it smelled. "Thanks. I didn't think to caffeinate."

"Amateur mistake. Those parents and their cherubs will eat you alive if you aren't operating at one hundred percent."

He opened his mouth to defend the people of the town he'd come to think of as home, but the smile on her face told him she was only playing. She seemed to enjoy teasing. Odd—it didn't fit his image of her. He chugged half the drink. Took a deep breath then let it out. "Ready to do this?"

"Absolutely." She stretched as tall as her five-foot-three frame could and strutted forward. She glanced over her shoulder. "You coming?"

He closed his mouth and strode beside her. "You're good at this."

"Just playing the part." She raised her chin slightly and coolly walked past all the waiting children and teens.

Playing the part? Was anything about her real? He'd thought she was genuine, and that everyone had been wrong about her, but maybe he'd judged her too quickly.

This woman definitely fit the way the tabloids had described her.

Who was the real Estelle Rogers?

He stopped at the front of the line, stuck two fingers between his teeth and let out a shrill whistle.

Excited chatter died down.

"Thank you. We're trying something different this year. Please follow Ms. Rogers and me inside. You will register as you enter the auditorium. Auditions will be held in front of everyone." It was a good thing he had several volunteers waiting to get all the kids checked in. Hopefully they'd be able to process everyone within the hour he'd allotted.

A murmur erupted.

He whistled again. "If anyone has a problem with this format, feel free to leave now." He wanted to weed out the kids who fought stage fright, and the best way to do that was to throw them into the spotlight during auditions. If they froze then he'd know not to cast them in a large role. He'd made that mistake last year and refused to put any child or teen through that again.

Estelle's boots clicked on the tile-floored hallway. "Well done," she whispered.

He stood a little taller. "Thanks." He pulled open the door. "After you."

She nodded and walked to the front. He'd had one of the older teens come in early to get the auditorium ready. Everything was exactly as he'd requested.

The volunteers were efficient, but they still started a

little late.

~

Two hours into the auditions Estelle slid a note to him.

Take five?

He nodded and raised his hand for the girl singing to stop. He'd heard enough. Why would the parents of someone who was tone-deaf allow their child to audition for a musical? He scribbled a note to remind himself she must be an extra with no singing parts. "Thank you." He stood and faced everyone who was still waiting. "We're going to take a break." He glanced at his watch. "Let's be back in fifteen minutes."

Estelle rose and discreetly stretched. "Why do you do this? From what I've seen, this town is in need of talent."

He frowned and pulled her toward a side exit so no one would hear their conversation. "It's been a rough start, but we only need three good singers. The rest are in the chorus or won't have a speaking part at all."

"Okay, but that last girl couldn't dance or sing if her life depended on it. How's that going to work in a musical?"

"She's a kid. Be nice. I anticipated we'd have some with two left feet. I've hired an excellent local choreographer. She's great with kids." There was no way he'd allow this production to be a flop. The theater had been his wife's passion—he owed her this. If it wasn't

27

for him . . . No. He needed to stop going there. Trinity had loved working with the children because they were so genuine. In many ways, he'd begun this summer theater as a tribute to his late wife and daughter. They were both triple threats—singing, dancing, and acting. He didn't have an ounce of talent when it came to those things, but he knew talent when he saw it.

"I didn't mean to be unkind." Estelle's blue eyes darkened. "Helen told me everyone who auditions gets a part, and I panicked."

He patted her shoulder, sending a tingle zipping up his arm. He yanked his arm to his side. "Leave the panicking to me. I need some air." He moved toward the exit leading to the alley.

Estelle two-timed it after him, her heels giving away her haste. She spoke in a loud whisper. "Stop running from me."

He pulled up short and turned to face her. "What?"

"Why the rush? You gave everyone fifteen minutes. There's plenty of time."

He shrugged. No way would he admit to trying to create a little space between them. That tingle bothered him big time. He couldn't be attracted to Estelle Rogers. Even though he wanted to honor his wife and daughter's memory with this children's theater, he could never get involved with an actress again. Especially one Trinity had disliked.

He raised his face toward the sky, soaking in the sunrays that shone through the parted clouds and breathing in deeply of the warming air.

"Are you just going to stand there?" Estelle asked. She placed her hands at her waist and tapped her foot. "You were rushing a minute ago."

"I wanted some fresh air. Relax, Hollywood. We take things a little slower here."

Her brow puckered. "Don't call me that."

Whoa. Someone was a little sensitive. "Sorry. I suppose we could head back, since you're in such a hurry," he teased. "We'll need to walk around to the front. These doors are locked from the outside." He glanced at his watch. More time had passed than he realized. He increased his stride.

"Oh. We could have put a stopper in the way." She kept pace beside him as he walked through the alley and toward the front of the building. Coming out here had been stupid, except he'd been trying to get away from her. A lot of good that did. Now they'd both be late. They finally reached the front of the big building, and he held the door for her.

"Thanks." She picked up the pace once they were inside then breezed into the auditorium.

He clapped his hands together. "Okay, everyone! Let's get going." He sat and flipped his clipboard right side up. "Jenny Denton," he called out, "you're up."

Jenny ran onto the stage. She opened her mouth, beginning the theme song for the musical. A hush fell over the room. Her voice, clear and strong, graced each note with perfection. She pirouetted across the stage and ended with a leap at exactly the right moment. She was a triple threat. His shoulders tightened.

Estelle leaned in close. "Looks like we found our lead."

"Maybe." He wasn't ready to commit. She was exceptional, but seeing her up there reminded him so much of Kendal. They could be sisters, their appearance was so similar. How would he survive the summer if Jenny played the lead? It was going to be hard enough having her in the musical at all, but if she played Cindy he'd be working with her constantly.

"What's the matter?" Estelle asked as everyone applauded.

"Nothing." How could she always tell when he was upset? His job had gotten a lot harder. He suspected there would be several angry moms on Monday when he posted the parts. This very well might be his last summer with the theater.

3

"How can you say Jenny isn't the one?" Estelle paced the width of the stage with a hand resting on her hip. "Did we sit through the same audition?" She didn't bother to temper her frustration. Blake was being a stubborn mule about this, which made no sense considering he had to want the best person for the part. She'd heard of being a control freak, but this was ridiculous.

Blake scrubbed a hand up and down his face as he sat at a table with pictures of all the kids spread out in front of him. "She doesn't have the look I was going for."

"So what? Jenny Denton was born to play Cindy Stetson." She crossed her arms and tapped her foot. "You know as well as I do that I'm right. Come on, Blake. What gives?"

"She lacks experience."

"It's children's theater! What do you expect? She's not going to have a lifetime of credits to her name."

Blake stood and strode toward the doors in the back of the auditorium. "I need a break."

"You've got to be kidding me," she muttered. What was wrong with that man? They could have been out of here hours ago, but instead it was after nine on a Friday night and they still hadn't finished casting. She stepped down the side stairs and strolled over to the table Blake had occupied.

Three pictures grabbed her attention—Paris, Jenny, and Melody, the girl whose mom had given Blake a difficult time. All the girls were close in age and talent, but Jenny could sing circles around the others.

The door to the auditorium opened and Helen scooted in. She raised a brown sack. "I brought provisions." She strode toward the table. "Where's Blake? I thought he'd be in here with you."

"He took a break." Estelle sighed and sat in an auditorium chair.

Helen joined her at the table and pulled out roast beef sandwiches. "What's wrong?"

"How long have you known Blake?" Maybe the older woman could offer some insight on why he was being so difficult.

"My goodness. He and Derek have been friends since they were kids. I feel like I've known him his entire life. I suppose I'm like a second mother to him."

"I had no idea. You never said anything."

Helen shrugged. "There was no reason to. Why all the questions?"

"I'm trying to figure him out. He wanted my help with casting, yet he won't let the best person for the role have it."

Helen frowned. "That doesn't sound like Blake. Who's this person you want?"

Estelle slid Jenny's photo over to Helen.

She gasped. "Oh my goodness. She looks so much like Kendal."

"Who's Kendal?"

"She was my daughter." Blake towered over them. His brow bunched as if he was in pain.

Estelle jumped. "You're like a ninja or something." He had a daughter? Wait, he said *was*. Could that be what was causing them to butt heads?

"Thanks for the food, Helen. I can always count on you to take care of me."

Helen took his hand and gave it a quick squeeze before letting it go. "You know it." She stood and slipped her arm through her purse. "The two of you have been here all day. Maybe a change in scenery would help this process move along."

Blake let out a long sigh. "You might be right." He glanced at Estelle. "You okay with moving this to the farm?"

Estelle couldn't believe he'd agreed. When she'd made the same suggestion two hours ago he'd refused. Go figure. "It's fine." She quickly gathered everything into a pile and slid it all into her oversized purse. During the auditions earlier she'd taken notes about who she would cast in each of the roles. She figured they'd have been out of here in under an hour, but Blake clearly had an emotional connection to this musical and these kids, so it was personal for him.

They headed out together. She walked to Helen's car, which was parked right outside the door. "You got lucky. I had to park a block away."

"Hop in. I'll give you a ride to your car."

"Thanks." She climbed in and buckled up. "Make a left at the next intersection. I'm parked about halfway up the block."

"Okie-dokie." Helen pulled away from the curb. "I haven't seen Blake like this since he first came to live in Oak Knoll four years ago. I'm worried about him."

"Aren't you the one always telling me not to worry and quoting scripture?"

"True, but when someone you care about is hurting, that practice is easier in theory," she said drily. She turned at the intersection.

"I hear that." *Lord, we both know I'm self-centered, and I'm really not asking this for me. I'm concerned about Blake. Please help him through whatever is going on in his head. Thanks.*

Helen had taught her so much about turning her troubles over to the Lord that it had begun to become second nature, except for one thing. Although she was good at the praying part, the letting go part was tough.

Helen pulled over. "That looks like yours."

"Yes. Thanks." Estelle got out and walked to her car. Except for the streetlights, the town was dark. It seemed Oak Knoll went to bed early. She waited for Helen to pull out then followed her to the farm. She parked in front of the barn beside Blake's pickup.

Helen got out of her car. "I imagine Blake will want to work in there." She motioned toward the barn. "There's lots of room to spread out, and the cottage is a little cramped."

"Okay. He's probably already inside," Estelle said. "Good night."

"'Night. I'll pray the two of you can get this figured out sooner than later."

"I appreciate that. I'll be praying too."

Estelle slid the barn door to the side, noting the lights shone bright.

Blake balanced a table on its side. He pulled the legs out, flipped it upright, and looked in her direction. "You ready to finish this?"

"Maybe we should wait until morning." It had been a long day. If Blake had time to sleep on it, he might be more likely to see things her way.

"No. I want to nail this down tonight. It won't take long."

With a sigh, she stepped further into the well-kept barn. The scent of fresh hay filled the air.

Blake pulled two metal chairs over to a long banquet-sized table. "We can work here."

She pulled the audition photos out of her bag and placed them on the table. "Before we begin, I'm curious about something."

He shot her a wary look.

"You said Jenny looks like your daughter. Is that why you don't want to give her the lead?"

He sat quiet for a moment, as if lost in thought then stood. "I'll be right back." He moved into a room off to the side and returned a moment later holding a framed picture. "That was my wife, Trinity, and my daughter, Kendal."

She took the framed photo. Jenny resembled his daughter but only slightly. They both had long, dark hair and a sweet smile. Estelle looked a little closer. Their eyes were similar too. His wife didn't look like their daughter at all, though. She must take after her dad. Trinity had long, wavy blonde hair. Her green eyes were gorgeous. And her face was perfectly heart-shaped. She was stunning.

"They're beautiful." She handed him the photograph. Clearly he wasn't going to answer her question about why he wouldn't give Jenny the lead.

"Thanks." He set it on the table. "You met Trinity once."

"I did?" When she saw the anger that filled his eyes, she recoiled—as if he struck her. Why was he so angry? She was afraid to hear what he would say but needed to know. It was no secret she hadn't been the kindest person once upon a time. It wasn't until she'd met Helen and been introduced to the Lord that she'd begun to change her ways and treat people with kindness and respect. Helen had gently pointed out that her reactions to people could use some work. She was ashamed of the way she'd behaved but couldn't take back her past. It would always be there. "Tell me about it."

"My daughter was a big fan of yours, and Trinity had a small part in *Tide of Love*."

"The last decent movie I starred in." Estelle remembered well the summer they'd filmed that movie—record high temperatures had made it miserable. In spite of the uncomfortable heat, she'd been full of herself, riding high on her success.

He nodded. "She asked for your autograph for Kendal. You refused and gave Trinity the brush-off."

Regret washed over Estelle. No wonder he had seemed wary of her when they'd first met. "I'm sorry. I know it's too little too late. There's no good excuse for my behavior."

"At least we can agree on one thing."

She winced. "Ouch. What were your wife and daughter like?"

He shuffled through his notes as if he hadn't heard her.

She narrowed her eyes and clenched her hands together. She had enough to deal with without taking on Blake too. Now that she'd had time to think things through, she felt badly about Jeff and needed to figure out how to make amends with him. Not that she wanted to get back together. He was right—if she truly loved him, saying yes to his proposal would have been easy. She would miss him though. He was a good man, and she enjoyed spending time with him. She especially enjoyed his cooking. But Jeff was in California, and Blake was here. She pushed her thoughts aside and focused on him. "I understand not wanting to tell me about your wife and daughter, and I understand why you don't like me, but I'm here to help. If you don't want it, I'll leave."

The angry look on his face softened, and he blew out a breath. "I'm sorry. That comment was uncalled for, but I'd rather not talk about Trinity and Kendal anymore."

"Should I leave?"

"No. Helen is right. I need you." He rubbed the back of his neck. "I think I'm stalling. Whatever we decide, there will be at least a few disappointed kids and possibly angry parents to deal with."

"Wimp," she teased.

His eyes narrowed.

She raised her hands. "I was teasing. I'm a different person now. If you give me a chance, I can prove it."

Indecision crossed his face then cleared. "I suppose that's only fair."

~

Blake flicked a pencil back and forth between his fingers. He hadn't meant to tell Estelle about her connection to his wife. His intent had been to stuff his bias aside and do as Helen had suggested—take advantage of Estelle's experience. Instead he'd made a mess of things. If they were going to work together, he could put in a little effort to get to know her as she requested. "So tell me about yourself. Who are you?"

Surprise lit her eyes. "For starters, I'm actually a nice person most of the time." She shot him a wry grin. "My life is wrapped up in my restaurant. I was dating my executive chef until he proposed. It's over now."

"You broke up with him because he proposed?" What kind of person did that? She wasn't gaining any points to his way of thinking.

She shook her head. "No. He broke up with me the day I got here."

"I'm confused."

"I had told him I needed time to think. Being the smart man that he is, he realized that if I truly loved him, I'd have been able to give him an answer. I couldn't. So after a week of waiting, he broke up with me over the phone."

"Are you okay?"

"I will be. I feel horrible because I know he's hurt. But I'm not brokenhearted." She shrugged. "Okay, maybe I'm a little sad, but it's for the best."

When he'd asked her to tell him about herself, this was the last thing he'd expected to hear. Clearly she was more open than he'd realized. Her transparency shocked him and drew him to her at the same time.

He picked up the photos of Paris and Jenny. If he were honest, Jenny was perfect for the role of Cindy.

Her acting skills weren't as strong as her singing, but he had no doubt she'd bring Cindy to life on the stage.

He looked up and met Estelle's eyes. "Jenny can play Cindy."

"Really?" The sadness from a moment ago cleared. She leaned forward. "Just like that?" She snapped her fingers.

His breath hitched. Her eyes shone, and she seemed more beautiful than she had when they'd first met. How was that possible? "Yes. You inspired me to look past my own insecurity and pain." He dipped his head. "Now what did you think of Melody and Paris?" She seemed to take his comment in stride—good. He didn't want to make a big deal about his decision.

"Paris has exceptional stage presence, but Melody's rawness makes her perfect for the role of Anna."

"I agree." Although he hadn't thought of it until she pointed it out. "I wonder if that will be good enough for her mother?"

"Why does it matter?" She flipped her hair over her shoulder.

"It matters because she donates a great deal of money every year, and I depend on her donation to cover the cost of building the set."

"Hmm." Estelle pressed her pink lips together. "Let me handle Mrs. Smith."

Ten minutes ago he would have argued, but now that he'd had a glimpse of the real Estelle he had confidence in her. "Gladly."

He had no idea what she had in mind, and he didn't want to know. Once they came to an agreement on those two roles, the rest were easy. Because of the large turnout, he'd have to add a few extras in the crowd scenes. So long as there was enough room on the stage, it would all work out.

Estelle stretched catlike and yawned. "I'm glad tomorrow is Saturday, and I have nowhere to be. This was quite a day."

Today had felt like a week's worth of work rolled into one. "Wish I had a day to relax too. If the weather holds, I have a house to paint."

"Have fun with that." She headed toward the door.

"Wait."

She turned.

"Practice is Monday through Friday, nine to noon. Extra rehearsals will be added as needed. Beginning this week. I'll update the website tomorrow so everyone knows their part."

"It occurred to me that you missed casting one role."

"The stepmother?" No one had auditioned for the role. He'd been formulating a Plan B but wasn't sure what she'd think.

Estelle nodded.

"Actually." He swallowed hard. "I was kind of hoping you—"

She raised a hand. "No way."

"Come on, Estelle. The kids need you." He held his

breath. "I need you." Without the stepmother role filled, they had no musical.

Her eyes widened before she pivoted and fled the barn.

He didn't mean to upset her. He would have thought she'd jump at the chance to play the role. She'd said herself that she needed something to fill her time this summer. Now what would he do? His remake of the classic *Cinderella* wouldn't work without a mother, and none of the teen girls could pull off that part. There was another option, but Derek might not agree.

~

Blake had clearly lost his mind if he thought for one minute she'd actually be in his musical. She had been clear that her acting days were over.

Estelle slammed the cottage door and plopped down on the couch. Her feet throbbed. She peeled off her boots. No one had warned her how long this day would be. She would've been better off in sneakers and jeans.

Her phone buzzed. She checked the caller ID. "Kayla? Is everything okay?"

"I was going to ask you the same thing. Blake called Derek and begged him to talk to you. He told him no and hung up then promptly fell back to sleep before I could question him. What's going on?"

"So you don't know?"

"I'm clueless. I'm losing my beauty sleep, but as long as I'm awake, please enlighten me."

Estelle filled her in. "Do you think this was all some setup to get a former celebrity here to give a boost to his little theater?" If that was the case, she regretted being so open with him about her personal life. It seemed she lacked the ability to judge character. This was why she allowed so few people to get close to her. She'd trusted Helen's judgment, though.

"No way were you set up. I know Blake pretty well, and I'm confident that was never his intention. Helen, on the other hand, is a different story. But not for the reason you think. She loves Blake like a son and you like a daughter. If, and that's a big if, this was all part of her plan, then it was made out of love and not intended to hurt you."

Of course Kayla was right. Helen had mentioned she thought of Blake like a son, and in the six years she'd known the woman, she'd never given Estelle a reason to doubt her. "Wait, what does Helen have to do with this?"

"Everything. She thinks you gave up on acting and believes if you're in the musical, word would travel, and it would jumpstart your acting career again. And at the same time it would boost Blake's visibility as a writer."

"Okay, but why would she think any of that?" Estelle had never thought of Helen as someone who would manipulate people, but it seemed once again she'd misjudged a person.

"She's a big fan of yours. I guess she wants to see

you on the silver screen again."

Estelle sighed. "I never would've suspected Helen of doing something like this. She's my friend, and I trusted her."

"You still can. But now you know her motives. She thinks very highly of you, and she's proud of the person you've become."

Estelle warmed at the kind words, but at the same time frustration and confusion plagued her. Helen knew why she'd given up acting. This made no sense. "Thanks for telling me."

"I thought you should know. So you had no idea Blake wanted you to play the stepmother?"

"Not a clue. I figured one of the kids would do it. After all, it's a *children's* theater."

Kayla yawned.

"I'm keeping you up. I'm sorry. Let's talk tomorrow."

"Are you sure?"

"Yes. I need time to think and process anyway."

"I'm taking the girls to the park Sunday afternoon. Maybe you could meet us."

"I'd like that. It's about time too. I only know them from pictures." They firmed up their plan to meet then disconnected the call. Maybe by the time Sunday rolled around she'd have a better grasp on things.

Overwhelmed with everything that had been thrown at her this week, Estelle closed her eyes and rested her head against the back cushion. What would be next?

4

Derek looked past Blake toward the church exit. "Kayla and the girls will be waiting. You know it's tradition for us to go out for lunch on Sundays after church."

"This will only take a minute," Blake said. "Have you given any further thought to asking Kayla to play the stepmother?"

Derek frowned. "I'm not asking her, but if you want to, go for it. I can tell you what she'll say, though. Our daughters are her priority."

"I have to try." He clapped Derek's shoulder. "I better find her before you leave."

"She's probably outside."

Blake nodded and moved toward the glass doors that led to the parking lot. Kayla was off to the right. Her daughters chased each other in circles around Kayla and the woman she was talking with. He waited until they were finished and the other woman turned to walk away. "Excuse me, Kayla. Do you have a minute?"

"Sure. What's up?"

"I'm sure you've heard that I'm looking to fill the role of the stepmother with an adult for the kids' theater."

She nodded.

"I asked Estelle, but she said no. I'm hoping you'll consider taking the role."

"Me?" she squeaked. "I'm not an actor."

"No, but you are a great singer, and with a little coaching from Estelle . . ." He held his breath. He had to get this nailed down today, and he didn't know who else to ask.

She shook her head. "I'm sorry, Blake. My life is full with these two kiddos. I don't see how I could possibly work a musical into it." She reached down and captured her youngest, drawing her into her arms and holding her close. "Are you sure about Estelle? We talked on Friday night. I thought maybe given time to mull it over, she might change her mind."

"If she did, she didn't tell me." In fact she was nowhere to be found all day yesterday, and he'd kept a lookout for her. "Are you sure you won't consider the role? I know how much you love music, and I suspect you have the entertainment bug. Maybe Derek could help out with the girls for a couple of hours each day." He'd seen her sing in concert with her husband, and if the look on her face could be believed, she thoroughly loved performing for a crowd.

"He probably would if I asked, but I'm not going to."

He hated to sound so desperate, but he was. This musical would not work without the stepmom, and he didn't have time to do a rewrite. He hadn't thought it would be so difficult to fill the spot. The announcement in the paper even talked about the role. He'd thought for sure at least a few women would audition, maybe even one of the kids' moms. "Please think about it over lunch. Talk to Derek and then get back to me. Please, Kayla. I don't know who else to ask."

"Fine. I'll bring it up at lunch, but honestly, I can't see my answer changing." She moved Mae to her hip and grasped Betsy's hand.

"Thank you. I appreciate this. I'd owe you big time if you decide to do it."

"Yes, you would. Come on, girls. I see Daddy. Blake, I'll text you with my answer after we're done eating." The happy trio walked toward Derek.

Sadness swept over him. That was once him waiting on his wife and daughter. He shook off the sorrow that snuck up on him. It was time to move past the melancholy that often gripped him at the most unexpected times. He missed his family, even though it had been five years since they'd died in a car crash on the way to Kendal's commercial audition. He'd been late getting home with the car, and Trinity was beside herself. He should have driven them himself like she had asked, but instead he stayed home and let her drive. Then they might still be here. It was his fault they weren't. Guilt pressed down on him.

"Hey there." Estelle stopped and looked at him with concern in her eyes. "Are you okay?"

He buried his thoughts and focused on Estelle. "I'm fine. I'm glad to see you. Did you change your mind about the part?"

She chuckled. "You're relentless. No, I haven't. You sure you're all right?"

"Positive." He forced a smile.

"Then I need to go. Kayla invited me to lunch with her family at the diner." She shrugged a shoulder. "Kind of strange too, since we were planning to meet in the park later. See you." Her spiky shoes clicked on the pavement as she strode toward her car. He should tell her it'd be faster to walk since parking would be scarce, but considering her choice in footwear, he stayed quiet.

Too bad he didn't have any spy gear. He'd love to be privy to their lunch conversation. Would Kayla try to talk Estelle into playing the role? He looked around the rapidly emptying parking lot. He should head home and grab a bite. Then he had work to do.

Pastor Miller strolled over to him wearing a cabbie style hat over his bald head. Probably trying to keep the sun off. "How's it going, Blake?"

"You know how it is this time of year."

He nodded. "I heard about the auditions. Rumor has it Jenny Denton is playing Cinderella."

"Word travels fast." He shouldn't be surprised the pastor knew, since he seemed to keep up on all that was going on in the small town.

"That children's theater is the most exciting thing in Oak Knoll this time of year." He grinned. "I never imagined a brunette Cinderella."

"Me neither." Paris had long blonde hair—one of the reasons he'd wanted her in the role. "But Jenny can always wear a wig if we decide the public isn't ready for a brunette Cinderella. Considering my Cinderella goes by Cindy, I think we'll be fine."

Pastor Miller chuckled. "I hadn't thought of that. Do you have lunch plans? My wife and I are barbecuing." He patted his ample stomach. "You're welcome to join us. There's always more than enough food."

Blake hesitated. Pastor Miller and his wife had never invited him over, although he'd been attending the church for the past four years. Why now? "Sure. Thanks. May I bring anything?"

"Just yourself. Come over anytime. Merry is already at home getting things ready."

"All right then. I'll see you soon." At the very least, lunch with the Millers would be a nice distraction— much better than sitting at home coming up with a re-write for the musical while waiting to hear from Kayla.

~

Estelle sat with the Wood family at their favorite diner.

Mae wrapped her tiny fingers around Estelle's wrist. "I wike you hair. So pitty."

Mae clearly had trouble with l's and r's. "Thank you. I think your hair is pretty too." She tugged gently on one of the child's brunette pigtails.

Mae giggled. "Mommy does that."

"She does, huh?" Estelle shot a look toward Kayla. Who would have thought they could actually be friends, considering their history? Kayla was one of the most forgiving people she'd ever met.

"She's right. I can't resist tugging on a pigtail." Kayla reached out toward her older daughter and pulled softly on her hair.

Betsy frowned and brushed her mother's hand away. "Don't, Mommy. I not wike that."

"I *don't* like that," Derek corrected.

Their food arrived, and the girls dug into their mac and cheese. Estelle eyed her choice of a Cobb salad compared to the other adults' burgers, fries and chocolate shakes. Regret hit her, but there was nothing to be done about it now. "As much as I love crashing your Sunday tradition, I have a feeling you invited me for a reason, considering we were already planning to meet up later."

Kayla nodded. "You're right. Blake asked me to play the role of Cinderella's stepmother. I told him no, but he convinced me to talk to Derek and reconsider it over lunch. Since you're involved too, I wanted to include you in the discussion."

Estelle leaned in. "You're seriously considering it?" She didn't know her friend had any aspirations for the theater.

"I'm not sure if I am or not, but I want to be open to the idea. He's clearly desperate, or he never would have come to me."

He asked Kayla to play the role? Somehow Estelle thought he'd try to coerce her into it. Instead he respected her answer. *Hmm*. Not what she'd expected, at all.

Her salad looked even less appetizing now than it had a moment ago. What was her problem? She'd been upset when she thought Helen or Blake were trying to take advantage of her celebrity status, but when they moved on to Plan B, she felt put out. "What would you like to do, Kayla? Do you want to spend the summer in the theater with a bunch of kids that aren't yours?"

"My gut response was I don't have time, but then I thought maybe it could work with Derek's help."

His eyes widened. "You're seriously considering it?"

Clearly her husband thought she'd turn the part down. Guess Derek didn't know his wife as well as he thought. But how well does anyone know another person married or not? Doesn't everyone have secret dreams?

"I'm not sure," Kayla said. "I want to help him, but I don't know about being in a musical." She ducked her chin then tilted her head to the side. "When I was a kid we went to New York and watched a couple of Broadway musicals. From then on I wanted to be in one. I loved everything about them. But we didn't have a theater here back then."

"You could have gone to Salem," Derek said.

"I suppose, but I didn't want to bother my parents."

Of course she didn't. Kayla was never one to put others out. That was probably why she'd forgiven Estelle for being such a twit when they'd first met.

"Honey, if this is something you want to do," Derek said, "then I will support you. The girls and I can manage a few hours a day on our own. Right?" He looked to his daughters.

Betsy nodded, but Mae seemed oblivious.

"That's good to know. Thanks." Kayla bit down on her bottom lip then turned to Estelle. "I have another problem and it's big. I don't know how to act."

"Have you ever tried?" Estelle asked.

She shook her head. "Not really. There's always a little acting involved with singing, but it's not the same thing as performing in a musical."

"That's true. Plus you'd be playing a mean person. You'd have to work hard on your acting skills for this role." Estelle pressed her lips together. She didn't want to insult Kayla, but the woman was super nice, and she couldn't picture her being mean to anyone.

"Could you help me?" Kayla asked.

"Absolutely. But are you sure this is what you want to do? Once you commit, there's no backing out. We'd need your all from you." Listen to her. She sounded like she had a stake in the musical when all she'd been asked to do was help with casting. Then again, if she was going to coach Kayla, she'd be quite involved.

Kayla frowned. "I don't think I could give my all."

"Why not?" Derek asked. "I'll run lines with you, and you already know the music. You have my complete support if this is what you want. I know you can do this."

A mix of emotions played across Kayla's face then cleared. She looked to Estelle. "Okay. I'm in, but with a condition."

Estelle beamed a smile toward her friend. Though a little jealous, she was proud of her for taking the leap. Kayla had talent. She'd heard her sing multiple times with her husband. They both had the entertainment bug. Derek had planned to retire from performing but found it impossible after two years and wound up doing a mini-tour every year. Apparently, Derek AKA DJ Parker still sang to sellout crowds.

"What's your condition?" Derek asked.

"I need an understudy."

"I didn't think of that." Estelle's shoulders slumped. "We don't have one. No one else auditioned for the part."

"You could be my understudy."

Estelle gasped. She hadn't been anyone's understudy since middle school.

Derek chuckled. "I think you took her by surprise, Honey. I doubt Estelle Rogers has ever been anyone's understudy."

Kayla's cheeks turned a pretty pink. "I'm sorry. I

didn't mean to offend you."

"It's fine. I'm not offended. Just taken aback. I'm not much of a singer."

"Not true," Derek said. "I've heard you. You sing on key with good tone quality. You could totally pull off the songs. They aren't difficult."

"I gave up show business. I own a restaurant now."

He nodded. "A restaurant that appears to be running fine without you. Plus, you and I both know you have one more show in you."

Could he be right? She'd stopped acting because the parts stopped coming in, not because she hated it. Blake and Derek's musical was well written, and from what she'd heard of the score, the music was incredible. Plus Derek seemed to have the Midas touch when it came to writing hits.

She looked to Kayla. "Do you promise to give this your best and do everything in your power to be at all the rehearsals and performances?"

"How many performances are we talking about?"

"There are three performances over a weekend at the end of the summer. One on Friday night, one matinee on Saturday and then the final performance that night," Estelle said.

Kayla nodded slowly and looked to her husband with a raised brow. "What do you think?"

"It won't be easy, but with my mom's help we can make this work." He looked to Estelle. "That is, if *you* meet your end of the deal. You must be her understudy and coach her."

"I'll do it." The words rushed from her mouth. She needed to get out of here. She felt like the walls were closing in. "Do you mind if I take my salad to go and pass on the park?" she asked Kayla. She needed time to process and she couldn't do it in this bustling diner.

"Not at all. I suppose I should skip the park too since rehearsal begins this week."

"No. Park." Betsy pounded a fist on the table.

"Young lady," Derek said, "that kind of behavior is not okay. *I* will take you to the park, but only if you mind your table manners."

Her eyes looked downcast. "Sorry, Daddy. Can we still go play?" she asked in a small voice.

"Yes." He grinned. "As soon as I finish my lunch."

Estelle got their waitress's attention and had her food boxed to go. "The practice schedule is online." She slid out.

"Okay. Thanks." Kayla scooted out of the booth and gave her a quick hug. "Thanks for agreeing to this. When we talked the other night, I never in my wildest imagination considered doing the part myself. Are you sure you're okay with everything?"

Estelle returned her hug. "I'm sure. I'll see you tomorrow."

She left the diner and ambled up the block to her car. What had happened in there? Had she really agreed to play the understudy of a role in a small-town children's theater? If the tabloids got hold of this, oh-boy! The town would be inundated with paparazzi, much like it had the last time she had been here, six years ago. No matter what, she'd do her level best to keep this quiet. The last thing she wanted was to be featured in a *Then and Now* segment on some television gossip show or celebrity magazine.

5

Blake's phone vibrated. He pulled it from his pocket and did a fist pump. Kayla had said yes! He could hardly believe it.

"Good news?" Pastor Miller asked from across the picnic table.

"The best. Kayla Wood agreed to play the stepmother in my musical." He took a long drink of lemonade then read the rest of the text. "No way."

Merry chuckled. "This is more fun than watching the Leroy twins pretend they're not passing notes during church. What has you so surprised?"

He looked up at the couple across the table from him. "Do you believe in miracles?"

Pastor scratched his neck. "You've been sitting in the Sunday morning service for years, and you seriously asked us that?"

"Good point." He raised his phone. "Estelle Rogers is the understudy."

Merry gasped and clapped. "That's incredible. This

little town is going to make the entertainment map—if you can get her on stage for at least one performance. Before you know it, we'll be raising funds for an auditorium where all the famous people who want to come here can perform."

Pastor patted her hand. "Let's not get ahead of ourselves. I'm proud of Kayla for taking a risk. Since she had her girls and sold her half of the florist business, she's practically become a hermit."

Merry nodded. "I only see her on Sundays now. I used to see her all over town at this or that meeting. But those girls consume her life."

"Well, it seems that's about to change." Blake shook his head. "I still can't believe it. How did Estelle and Derek convince Kayla to agree? She gave me a firm no about taking on the role."

"It's a woman's prerogative to change her mind," Merry stated matter-of-factly.

"I suppose so." Blake looked down at his mostly empty plate, grabbed what was left of his burger, then popped the last bite into his mouth. This news was almost too good to be true. He knew Kayla would never tease about such a thing, but it was still incredible. Blake looked to his hosts. "Do you mind if I eat and run? I have a lot of stuff to do today before rehearsal begins tomorrow." The most important thing he had to do was confirm the time the choreographer would be at the community center. They needed to get the dances marked out right away.

"Not at all. It was nice getting to visit with you today," Pastor said. "Merry and I started having a family over every Sunday after church. I suppose we should've been doing it for years now, but we just thought of it recently."

Blake stood. "Better late than never. I appreciate being asked." He also appreciated they hadn't invited any single women to try to set him up with. Sometimes well-meaning friends did that, and it was awkward for everyone. Today was refreshing. They were easy to talk to, and he'd found himself talking about things he never told people. Hopefully, he could trust them to keep his personal life to themselves. "I'll be seeing you."

The couple rose in unison, wearing matching smiles.

He'd always thought of them as rather serious people, but today had shown him another side. "'Bye." He made his way to the gate and then on to his pickup. Would Estelle be at the farm? Now that she was an understudy, she'd be around a lot more. He hadn't thought of that at first, and he was relieved to realize it didn't bother him at all. When they'd first met, he had wanted nothing to do with her because of the memories she brought to mind and because of what Trinity had said about Estelle, but now he only felt relieved and grateful to have her help. This musical was bound to be a success. Maybe it would create enough buzz to grab the attention of other directors. He'd love to make a living off his writing.

He drove straight home and went in search of

Estelle, bypassing the house and heading for the courtyard garden. She sat at the little table Helen had recently added. His heart pounded at the sight of her.

"Afternoon." He willed himself to calm down and schooled his face so he didn't come across as giddy. He almost laughed at the thought. When was the last time he'd felt giddy with excitement about anything?

"Hi, yourself."

"How was lunch?" He rocked up onto the balls of his feet then down a few times before stopping himself.

"Nothing like I expected." She motioned toward a box that lay open on the table.

"Looks like you're still eating."

"I am. We spent all our time talking, so I asked to have my salad boxed up. Plus I'm sure they needed some family time without me. I assume you've heard the news." She forked a bite of salad into her mouth.

"I have. Thanks for agreeing to coach Kayla."

"Well, if I'm going to be associated with this thing I want it to be great." She quirked a grin.

He chuckled at her teasing and stepped closer to the table, resting a hand on the chair opposite her. "May I join you?"

She nodded.

"Kayla also said you agreed to understudy for her."

"True. I suppose someone needs to be prepared to step in if necessary. But I pray it won't be necessary."

He sobered at the realization that Estelle wasn't happy about this turn of events like he was. "I understand. You're determined to stay off the stage, aren't you?"

She shrugged.

"Why? What are you afraid of?"

Her gaze slammed into his. "Nothing," she said with a defensive tone. "What makes you think I'm afraid?"

He gentled his tone, not wanting to cause another rift between them. "You stopped acting rather abruptly. I assumed something happened."

She placed her fork down and looked him squarely in the eye. "What happened was the biggest flop of my career, and then my manager was arrested for human trafficking. No one wanted to touch me." Her voice cracked, and she looked away.

His heart melted with compassion for her pain. The demise of her career had been big news when it happened. Even Trinity had talked about it. "But that was a long time ago. People have short memories. I'm sure you could work in movies again if you wanted to."

Her sad eyes looked back at him. "I don't think so. But thank you for saying as much. Hollywood has moved on without me."

Doubtful. If he were a betting man, he'd wager her stint this summer would be exactly the kick in the pants she needed to start going out on auditions again. "Since you'll be at the theater anyway, would you be willing to help with a few things?"

"Of course. I already said I would help. Besides, I

have nothing better to do this summer."

He nodded. "Thanks." Helen had told him how Estelle had resisted volunteering. It looked like once she made up her mind to do something, she was committed—he liked that about her. He was beginning to wonder if Trinity's experience with her was a fluke. Then again, Estelle had admitted to not being the nicest. Regardless, he'd clearly judged her too harshly to begin with.

Tension flowed off her. "I need to know something."

"Okay." Unease settled over him at the serious look in her eyes.

"Was I invited to be a part of this production to draw attention to your musical?"

Where had she come up with that idea? He hadn't even wanted her help when they'd first met, and he'd been pretty clear about it. "No. I never even thought of that, but I suppose having you in the musical would be beneficial to ticket sales."

She studied his face. Looking for what? Her shoulders relaxed. He must have passed.

He should leave before he did or said something that would cause her to change her mind. "I have a lot to accomplish before tomorrow morning."

"The rest of my afternoon is free if you'd like help."

He hesitated. "I thought you had plans."

She shrugged. "They changed. What can I do?"

The eager look on her face that begged him to

accept her offer endeared her to him. He described everything on his to-do list.

"I think it'd be best if we divide and conquer." She rattled off several items she would take care of. "Since I'm going to be rehearsing the dance numbers, is there any place in town to buy dance shoes?"

He shook his head.

"Too bad." She pulled out her phone and started typing into it. "I'll have my assistant overnight mine. But Kayla is going to need a pair too."

"She's not the only one. There's a great dance supply place in Salem. I'll post the information on the theater's website. You want to carpool into town tomorrow?"

Surprise filled her face. "Sure. What time?"

"Seven."

She groaned. "Did I mention how much I dislike early mornings?"

"You'll survive." He had no doubt his words were true. He knew all about the schedules movie actors kept.

"Easy for you to say. You're probably a morning person."

"There's no probably about it."

"I should have known that's why you were such a bear the other night," she said playfully. "You'd better get a move on, General Price, or you won't finish that long list you created."

Remembering her response from when they'd started this journey together, he mimicked her, as he clicked his heels together and saluted her.

She laughed, and her blue eyes twinkled.

He sucked in a breath. She was stunning. No wonder Derek had fallen for her once upon a time.

"Blake?"

"Hmm?"

"Aren't you leaving?" She looked past him as if to say "go."

"Yes. I'm out of here. See you tomorrow." He'd better watch himself. The last thing he needed to do was get distracted by her. He had a musical to direct, and that would require all of his attention. Except one problem— Estelle would be at every rehearsal, and now that he realized she was actually a nice person, he couldn't get her out of his head.

~

Estelle gazed at her image in the full-length mirror at the cottage and held up a yellow sundress in one hand and a dove gray linen suit in the other. Today was the first day of rehearsals, and it would set the tone for the summer, so she wanted to present herself as a professional but also wanted to look approachable. The suit said professional, but linen would wrinkle. She tossed the suit aside and slipped the dress over her head.

A knock sounded at her door. She was late. "Coming." She slipped her feet into a comfortable pair of sandals, strode to the door, then pulled it open. Blake waited there holding daisies. A tingle zipped through her. "What are those for?" Surely Blake hadn't gotten her flowers. Clearly he was happy to have her help with the musical, but this was completely unnecessary. She opened her mouth—

"Helen asked me to hand deliver them. She's a morning person too and picked flowers at the crack of dawn." He winked as if he'd known what she was about to say.

Her face heated. Why would Blake bring her flowers? She should have known they'd be from Helen. "She spoils me. Hold on a second while I put them in water." She retreated to the kitchenette and pulled a glass from the cupboard. "You can come in while I take care of these." She flicked on the tap and filled the glass, then added the daisies. "These are one of my favorite flowers. They make me happy." She placed them on the table. "Ready?"

He nodded. "We need to get moving. I want to make sure we're the first ones there."

"I don't think that's going to be a problem. Doesn't rehearsal begin at nine?"

"Yes, but they start arriving by eight-thirty. Parents need to get to work."

"I should've thought of that, but we'll be fine." She trotted beside him to keep up. If he kept this pace all summer long, she'd never have to run on the treadmill again. "You could slow down a bit," she panted out the last words.

He dipped his head and looked at her with a chagrinned look. "Sorry. I get kind of nuts on day one."

"We all do, but some of us hide it a little better." She shot him a smile meant to relax him, but noted he only frowned. Tough crowd. Okay, so teasing wasn't a good idea today. Hopefully he'd chill before the kids arrived, otherwise he might freak out some of the more sensitive ones. She climbed into his pickup. "We can take my car tomorrow."

"I don't mind driving my pickup every day. That way if I have set pieces to drop off, I can."

She nodded and folded her hands in her lap, hoping to get a handle on her nerves. Veteran or not, it had been a long time since she'd had a first day on the set, and her tingling fingers testified to her uncharacteristic nerves. "You do this every summer?"

"Yep."

"Why?"

He shot a look her way. "What's with all the questions?"

She pressed her lips together and stared out the side window. She'd worked with directors like him before. Staying quiet was the best way to deal with them.

They rumbled toward town as cars zoomed in the opposite direction toward Salem. She was glad to be headed to Oak Knoll instead. The small town's charm had quickly grown on her. She hoped to be able to do a little shopping during their lunch break today—maybe even stop into Flowers and More and say hi to Jill.

Blake expelled a sharp breath. "I'm sorry for snapping. Mrs. Smith sent me an email. She won't be giving her usual donation this year."

What a difficult woman. "Why not? You gave her daughter a strong role."

"I said the same, but she won't be happy with anything less than Cindy."

"Well, that's not happening." Mrs. Smith might think she could control Blake with her money, but she'd learn the truth soon. Blake was a man who couldn't be bought. "How much does she usually donate?"

He rattled off an amount.

Wow. No wonder he's anxious for the money. "I know I said I'd deal with her and I will, but it would be nice if we weren't dependent on people like Mrs. Smith."

"I couldn't agree more. What do you suggest?"

It would be easy enough to get the funds for him from some of her philanthropic friends, but she believed people should work for what they had. "The kids can do a fundraiser to supplement the loss."

"They already do."

"Oh. You could raise ticket prices."

"Nope. They need to be affordable."

There had to be some way to have the funding they needed without the theater becoming dependent on one patron's donation. Maybe she should fill the gap this year, but that wasn't the point. The theater should be self-sufficient. "What about raising fees for the kids?"

"Impossible"

"Why? I mean, I get why you can't this year, but in the future you could."

"Summer theater is free for everyone. I don't want anyone excluded because of finances."

Free? "Please tell me you're joking. How do you keep the doors open? No wonder so many showed up for auditions." Even a nominal fee would go a long way toward covering expenses. "That has to change."

"No. It must be free." Blake's firm tone surprised her.

There had to be more going on here than she realized. It didn't make sense to not charge any kind of fee at all when it cost to run the theater. Did he receive a grant she didn't know about so they didn't depend strictly on donations and ticket sales? She'd make sure they had what they needed this year, but beyond that it should be solvent on its own.

She stared out the windshield as she debated with herself how to tell Blake her plan. Would he accept her money? Maybe she could make an anonymous donation. Yes. That was the way to go. She'd have her attorney wire the money, and no one would be the wiser.

Blake pulled up to the curb in front of the community center. "You ready for this?"

She tossed her shoulders back and raised her chin. "Oh yeah."

He grinned. "You're kind of cute when you're trying to be tough."

Pleasure shot through her. She made a face at him

then hopped out of the pickup. Her heart raced. *Get it together*. She was a professional. This was no big deal. She'd volunteered at the children's theater many times in LA. There was nothing to worry about. At least that's what she told herself.

6

Three hours into the first day of rehearsal, Estelle collapsed beside Kayla in the front row of the auditorium. "I had no idea how out of shape I've gotten."

"Tell me about it," Kayla said. "My feet hate me. I had no idea there'd be so much dancing involved. I'm not sure I'll survive the summer."

Estelle knew exactly how her friend felt. She'd never had to dance in a movie before, which was good since dancing wasn't her thing. Granted, they were mostly waltzing, but when you're not accustomed to it, whoo-boy it was tiring. "Rehearsals can be a killer, but by August, you'll have forgotten all about how you feel today."

"If I last that long." She turned to face Estelle. Concern filled her eyes. "I'm worried I won't be able to handle this. It's a lot."

"That's why we learn in small chunks. Look around you. The kids are tired too, but excitement radiates off of them." Which was exactly why she'd volunteered in LA. There was nothing like being around kids with their unfiltered joy of the arts. She was once like them, but time and experience had changed that.

"They do seem to be having fun." Kayla took a drink from her water bottle. "Did you do children's theater when you were a kid?"

"Only once, but it was the most fun I'd ever had. The acting bug bit me, and from that point on I was hooked."

"That's cool, and now you get to give back."

"I guess so, although I hadn't thought of being here like that." Too often her life revolved around her own universe—being here was good.

"I should head home and relieve Derek." Kayla stood.

"Wait." Estelle heard the panic in her voice and tempered her tone. "You'll be back tomorrow, right?"

"If I can move. Pray for me." She hobbled toward the exits.

Poor Kayla. "I will." She spotted Blake walking her way, and he didn't look happy. A groan escaped her lips. "Now what?" she whispered to herself.

Blake pointed toward the auditorium doors. "Did I see Kayla leave?"

Estelle nodded. This morning had been a challenge, even for her.

"But we weren't done with her." His brow furrowed.

"Well, she's done with us for today."

His frown deepened then cleared. "It's fine. You'll step in for her."

She pointed to the clock. "I'm done too."

He did a double take at the time. "I should've scheduled an all-day rehearsal." He whistled for everyone. Once the room quieted, he gave a short pep talk then dismissed the kids. "Why do I feel sick to my stomach?"

Estelle rested a hand on his shoulder. "It was the first day. Tomorrow will be better." Truthfully, today had been tragic. The kids were all over the place with their abilities, and they were missing two key volunteers who were on vacation.

"It can't get much worse." He ran a hand down his face.

She bumped her shoulder into the side of his arm. "Come on. Put on a positive face. Everyone takes their cue from you."

His features transformed into a smile that crinkled the skin around his eyes. "Better?"

"See. That wasn't hard." She tossed some encouraging words to the stragglers who were on their way out. Silence enveloped them—finally. She plopped back into a seat. "Wow. Just . . . wow."

Blake eased into the chair beside her. "Yep. We get off to a rough start every year, though, so I don't know why I panicked. Tomorrow is bound to get better."

Estelle chuckled. "You don't have to give me a pep

talk too. But I appreciate the effort." She reached over and gave his hand a quick squeeze.

A door at the back of the auditorium brushed open. Estelle looked over her shoulder. "It's Mrs. Smith," she whispered. "You want me to talk to her?"

"No. I will." A grim look crossed his face before he stood to face the woman.

Mrs. Smith stopped a few feet from them. "I've come to tell you that Melody won't be back."

"Why?" Estelle blurted before thinking.

"She's embarrassed to be playing one of the step-sisters. I know this isn't actually *Cinderella*, but everyone knows it's a remake, and it's insulting to be one of the ugly step-sisters."

Estelle shot a look to Blake, thinking he might want to respond, but he seemed to be at a loss for words, considering the dumbfounded look on his face. It was up to her.

"Melody is not ugly, nor will we make her be. As you stated this is *not Cinderella*, but rather inspired by it. Your daughter has a key role. I'm confused as to why she'd turn that down all because she's embarrassed? Some of the best roles ever were difficult and the characters were undesirable. That's what made the actors so amazing and why they won awards." Estelle couldn't help herself. If a person wanted to succeed in this business then they took the part offered. And this was a primo character.

Blake nodded.

Mrs. Smith stomped her foot. "My daughter had her heart set on playing Cindy."

Estelle held back a chuckle at the woman's theatrics. "I see. Well, as they say, there are no small parts, only small actors."

Mrs. Smith glared at her. "I thought having you here would be an asset—that you'd recognize talent when you see it. But—"

"Enough." Blake's voice silenced them both. "If leaving is truly what *Melody* wants, then fine."

"Mom," a shaky voice from the back called out. "I can do the part. It's fine. I don't have to be the star. I know you're disappointed, but it's fine. Really."

"Hush, Melody," her mother hissed.

Estelle strolled to the rear of the auditorium leaving Mrs. Smith and Blake at the front and found Melody sitting in the back row. She sat beside her. She kept her voice low. "Is it you or your mom who's having a problem?"

"My mom." Melody ducked her head. "It's so embarrassing."

Estelle patted her shoulder. "What can I do to help?"

Melody tilted her face and brushed her long hair out of her eyes. "Convince my mom that playing Anna is a great part."

"Actually, it is. Any idea why she's like this?"

Melody nodded. "She's trying to live out her own dreams through me. She wanted to be famous, but it never worked out for her."

Estelle finally understood what was going on. "Do you like acting, sweetie?"

The young teen shrugged. "It's all right, I guess. But I know I'm not that great."

At least one of the Smiths was in touch with reality. "Don't worry about that. I can help you with your acting, and Kayla, I mean Mrs. Wood, can help with your vocals. The best part of your role is that you can have fun with the vocals and your dancing can be silly. It's all in how you play the character. You can be creative with Anna—in fact, you could even upstage Cindy if you work hard enough."

"Really?"

"Mm-hmm."

"Thanks." She stood and scooted past Estelle then walked to where her mother and Blake were still arguing. "I want to play Anna. It will be fun. Please don't make me quit, Mom."

Estelle eased her way forward, curious to see how Mrs. Smith would react to her daughter's declaration.

"But you'll be the ugly step-sister."

"I don't have to be ugly. I can play up her personality in other ways." She looked to Estelle. "Right?"

"Sure. In fact, I like that idea. What do you think, Blake?"

"It could work. I look forward to seeing your interpretation of Anna."

Melody beamed. "Thanks!" She race-walked to the door.

"I guess that means she's in," Estelle said. "Can we count on your support this year, Mrs. Smith?"

The woman nodded and left without another word.

When the door whooshed shut, Estelle let out the breath she'd been holding to keep herself from laughing. "Did you see the color of her face?"

Blake smiled and raised his hand. "High-five. You did it. I don't know how, but you did."

She high-fived him, though she didn't share his elation. She felt for Melody and hoped the girl's mom didn't come down on her. "I wouldn't count on those funds yet. In fact, it might be wise to operate under a tighter budget."

He tipped his head to the side. "You might be right. She's kind of fickle, and I heard this morning from one of the other moms that she's in the middle of a nasty divorce. She might not even have the funds to donate."

It was as if Melody were living out Estelle's childhood, minus the overly dramatic stage mom. "I'm sorry to hear that. Poor Melody is probably stuck in the middle. I'm glad she decided to stay in the musical. It'll be a nice distraction for her."

"I agree. We make a good team, you and me. Now let's get lunch. I'm buying. You up for pizza?"

Her stomach lurched at his words. "Sounds good to me."

~

Friday afternoon, Blake stood in Helen's barn and looked at the prop for the mall food court scene Derek worked on. "We need to make sure the color is strong enough to be seen from the back of the auditorium."

"This isn't my first time painting. What are you so stressed about?" Derek dipped his brush in the paint tray.

"I want everything to be perfect, and I'm worried it won't be, thanks to our budget." Mrs. Smith had yet to drop off a check.

"Stop stressing. We've got this. There are enough volunteers to get this set ready with plenty of time to spare."

Derek was probably right. Several dads of cast members had offered to help with set design. "Your wife is doing a good job with her part."

Derek grinned. "I knew she would. Kayla doesn't do anything halfway. I'm still surprised she agreed to be in it, though. She's so devoted to our girls, it never occurred to me she'd say yes."

"Trinity was the same way until Kendal turned three, then she was ready to get back out there."

"Must have been the terrible threes."

"I thought it was the terrible twos," Blake said.

"Trust me, three is worse. At least it was with Betsy."

In no position to debate the issue, Blake grabbed a

paintbrush and dipped it in blue. It was funny how things changed. When they were younger, he was the one who wanted a family, and Derek had stars in his eyes with no thought of having a wife and kids.

"Reinforcements are here." Helen strolled into the barn with Pastor Miller and Merry, as well as the dance choreographer, Amber Jackson.

Speechless, Blake held his paintbrush midair. Pastor and Merry had never shown any interest in the children's theater. Why now?

"Welcome to the set brigade," Derek said. "Thanks, Mom."

"Sure thing. I'll bring out refreshments soon."

Blake finally found his voice. "How'd you know we needed help?"

Amber ambled closer. "Estelle mentioned it at rehearsal." She looked around. "She said she'd be here."

"One of the girls needed help with her lines, so she stayed late to help," Blake said.

Amber nodded. "When I told my aunt and uncle you needed help, they volunteered to offer a hand."

"Pastor Miller is your uncle?"

The trio laughed.

"He has a name," Amber said.

"He does? I mean, of course he does." Blake's face heated.

"I'm standing right here, folks. You're welcome to call me Joe. I'm sorry I didn't mention that years ago. I assumed you knew."

"It's fine and thanks, but I don't think I can call you Joe. To me you're Pastor."

Pastor chuckled. "I've heard that before. Whatever name you're comfortable with is fine, but if anything changes, you're free to use my given name." He looked around the barn. "This is a nice setup you have here." He focused on Derek. "When you mentioned you were painting the set, I had no idea what to expect."

Now it made sense why they were here—Pastor Miller was Derek's boss since he was the music minister. He must be making an effort to reach out to his employees outside of work. Probably for the same mysterious reason they were inviting families over to their place for Sunday lunch.

Derek put everyone to work painting the murals that would be the backdrops for various scenes. Each would be applied to a wall on wheels they used every year that was easy to move on and off the stage.

Amber laughed at something one of the Millers had said. Blake studied the choreographer. Her shoulder-length brown hair was swept up in a messy ponytail, her face was devoid of makeup, and her clothing choice of leggings with an off-the-shoulder top screamed dancer. He guessed she was probably twenty-five or twenty-six. It was still hard to believe she was the Millers' niece. He'd never noticed her at church. Of course, theirs wasn't the only one in town.

A shadow from the barn entrance dropped onto the canvas he was painting. He turned and shielded his eyes from the sunlight streaming in. Estelle stood there with her hair piled atop her head, holding a tray of sandwiches and wearing cutoffs and a T-shirt. She looked adorable but, more importantly, like she was ready to work. Good, they still had plenty to paint.

"Hi, Estelle. Grab a brush and jump in anywhere. Everything is numbered so you'll know what color to paint where." He'd done this enough years now that he'd finally figured out an efficient system.

"Great, thanks. Helen got sidetracked, but she'll bring out the rest of the snacks soon." She placed the tray on the table he'd set up the other night.

"This is almost like a church social," Merry said.

Amber's laughter bubbled up. "You think anything with food and people is like a church social."

"When she's right, she's right." Merry shrugged and resumed painting the backdrop for the diner scene. Although he'd used the classic *Cinderella* story, he'd modernized it to present day.

Helen entered the barn, struggling to carry a huge tray.

Blake rushed over to relieve her of it. "Let me help." He took the tray piled with fresh fruit and cheese and crackers to a nearby table.

"I'll be right back with lemonade and water." She left without waiting for a reply.

He'd better make sure she could handle both so she didn't have to make a third trip. "I'll help." He quickly caught up and strode beside her. "Thanks for doing this,

Helen. I know everyone appreciates your thoughtfulness."

"It's nothing. I feel like I'm contributing in my own way. Besides, I enjoy helping my boys out."

Blake draped an arm across her shoulder and gave it a light squeeze.

Helen patted his hand. "I was surprised to see Amber here. She's never helped out at one of these before, has she?"

"Nope. But this is the first year she's been involved in the theater. In the past we've kept it simple, and I did the choreography. She approached me about helping out because she opened a dance studio in town and is hoping to gain some students." He opened the door to the house and motioned Helen in ahead of him.

"How's Amber doing with the choreography?" Helen went to the kitchen.

"The steps are more involved than previous years." He chuckled. "Estelle and Kayla were dead on their feet the first day. I felt bad for them."

"Oh dear." She motioned toward another tray with two pitchers and stacked reusable cups. "I'm glad they didn't give up."

"Me too. The last thing I need is people quitting because the dances are too complicated." He turned and retraced their steps.

"How about the kids. Are they learning the routines okay?"

"Actually, they are. They're doing a lot better than I

could have hoped, considering how early it is in the summer."

"That's great. I'm proud of what you and Derek created." She pulled open the front door. "If you need anything else, you know where to find me."

"Thanks." He returned to the barn. Laughter rang out the open door. He stepped inside and set the drinks beside the snacks. "If anyone needs a break, the food is ready."

They set down their brushes and quickly cleaned up at the utility sink in the corner. Estelle plopped onto a bale of hay, drawing her knees to her chest.

"You don't want anything to eat?" Blake asked.

She held up a cup. "This is fine."

No wonder she was still model-thin. She didn't eat whenever food was around—he could learn from her example. He patted his middle. Then again, he was doing all right. He filled a cup with water, piled a plate up with food, then headed her direction. He eased onto a metal folding chair facing the hay bales. "How'd it go with Jenny?"

"Not bad."

He'd gotten to know Estelle well enough now to suspect she wasn't telling him everything. Had they made a mistake with the girl? Would she be able to do the role justice? Maybe he should have fought harder to have Paris play Cindy. He'd have to catch Estelle later when no one else was listening to find out what she was leaving out.

Amber sat in a chair beside him. "I can't thank you enough for giving me the opportunity to choreograph the musical. It's been a great experience so far."

His thoughts shifted gears to take in what Amber had said. "I'm glad. The kids seem to be enjoying themselves. Have you picked up any new students?"

Her face glowed as she nodded. "Several actually. I'm beyond pleased."

"Great." He munched on a grape.

Pastor and Merry joined them. "This sure brings back memories of our early days in ministry," Pastor said.

Merry nodded. "I kind of miss those days."

"Why's that?" Estelle asked.

"We were youth pastors, and the teens were so much fun. Granted, some could be a handful, but I'll never forget our time with them."

Pastor took his wife's hand and held it. "Oak Knoll Community Church was our first and only pastorate."

"Is that right?" Blake asked. "How long have you been here?"

"Twenty-two years," Pastor said. "We've had ups and downs, but this place is home." He looked toward Blake. "After bemoaning how busy everyone is and how disconnected we've started to feel from the church, we were challenged by friends to reach out to individual families and get to know them."

Merry nodded. "Take you for example, Blake. We see you every Sunday. Say hello and ask how you are, but that's the end of it. We know little about you or what makes you who you are. Sure we know the old timers, but not the younger generation."

"So," Pastor said, "we're doing our best to get involved and play a more active role in the lives of the people around us."

"Good for you," Derek said. "If we all did that, I think our sense of community would grow by leaps and bounds."

"Speaking of leaps and bounds, we should probably get back to work, so our progress can grow by leaps and bounds," Blake said.

Amber giggled and placed a hand on his forearm. "I like how you did that. Too funny."

He sat frozen, unsure how to respond. Was Amber flirting? He shot a look to Estelle for help.

She raised a brow and quirked a grin then stood. "Come on, Amber. Let's see who can finish their scene first." She wound her arm through Amber's, and mouthed, "you owe me" to him.

He'd never be able to pay Estelle back at this rate. She'd saved his hide with the musical, that much was certain, because no way would he have been able to pull it off without her expertise and assistance with the kids since this year's program was so much more complicated than anything he'd ever attempted. Who knew she'd volunteered at a children's theater in LA before and got along so well with kids and teenagers?

A crashing sound made him jump up and whirl around. *Oh no.*

7

Estelle blinked rapidly and slid the back of her hand across her face. Paint dripped off her chin and ran down her neck. She looked down at herself and groaned. Her clothes were likely ruined. She didn't know whether to laugh or cry. The barn had suddenly become deathly quiet. Heat flooded her body.

"Are you okay?" Blake rushed to her.

"I think so." Her knees hurt along with the palms of her hands from catching herself on the rough flooring.

"What happened?" Derek asked.

"I don't know. One minute I was walking over to dip my brush in a tray and the next, I was sprawled on the ground covered in paint."

"I'm so sorry," Amber said. "I think that was my fault. I set a paint can down, turned away for a second, and then you tripped."

"Landing in the paint trays we're using," Blake said with dismay in his voice.

She looked down and spotted a puddle of white

paint pooling on the barn floor. Bending over, she righted the can.

"Come on." Blake motioned toward the yard. "Let's hose you off."

Her heart warmed at his obvious concern, but worry nipped at her. "What about the floor? It's ruined." One more thing she'd have to figure out how to fix. She'd add it to her growing list. Today had been a rough day filled with unexpected issues. Including one at her restaurant.

"I'll take care of it," Derek said. "Don't worry, Estelle."

"Will your mom be upset?" She was afraid to hear the answer. Helen was the last person she wanted to cause problems for.

"No. She'll be fine. Trust me." Derek moved toward the utility sink. "I've got this. Go get cleaned up. By the time you come back, you'll wonder if you imagined the whole thing."

Amber chuckled. "I very much doubt that." She looked with compassion and regret to Estelle. "I'm so sorry that happened. I promise to be more careful."

"Don't worry about it." Estelle heard herself say without thinking. She'd sure come a long way. The last time something like this happened, she'd had the person who caused it fired. Now she felt bad about that, but there was nothing she could do to right her wrong all these years later. She headed for the hose outside in the yard.

Closing the door behind him, Blake followed her.

"You okay?"

"I'll live. Although I have a feeling I'm going to be sore. She looked down at her knees and noticed one was bleeding. *Great.* "I think I'm going to hide out in the cottage after I get the bulk of this paint off. I had something come up with my restaurant I should deal with, and clearly I'm too distracted to be working around the set."

"You do whatever you need to do, but you're more than welcome to join us if you change your mind. Accidents happen." He picked up the hose and turned it on. "It's going to be cold."

She shrugged and braced herself. A hard shot of spray hit her arms. She screamed.

Blake stopped. "Maybe you should just toss your clothes and go take a shower."

"No way. I love these cutoffs. Keep spraying." She squeezed her eyes shut and braced herself for the icy spray. It wasn't so bad once she got used to it, plus the sun warmed her, so that helped.

"I think I've got as much as will come off."

"Thanks. Guess I'll slosh my way to the cottage."

"I'll stop in later and see how you're doing."

"That's sweet but not necessary." She needed time alone to figure out what she was going to do about Jeff. She couldn't believe he'd given his two-week notice. That didn't give her much time to find a replacement. The worst part was she suspected he was leaving because of her. She should have known better than to date her executive chef.

Her feet squished in her sneakers as she wove around the side of the house and on into the courtyard. She slid her shoes off outside the door then made a mad dash for the bathroom to keep from dripping all over everything.

Once behind closed doors, she turned on the shower to as hot as it would go. Maybe she could melt away what was left of the paint. She imagined the scene that had played out in the barn. How had no one busted out laughing? Well, Amber had giggled. Come to think of it, Amber was probably the only one who'd witnessed her graceless fall. A chuckle escaped her lips. It *was* pretty funny. Amber had shown great restraint. Estelle stepped into the shower and laughed until her sides hurt. If someone had been filming, that clip would have gone viral for sure.

Later that evening, she sat on the couch, wearing sweats and a T-shirt with fluffy socks covering her freezing toes and worked on her laptop. The evening had cooled drastically. She pulled a soft blanket off the back of the couch and wrapped it around her shoulders. A knock sounded on the door. "Come in." She looked over her shoulder expecting to see Helen.

The door swung open. "You up for company?" Blake asked.

Her insides leapt. She'd forgotten he promised to check in on her. "Sure, come in and close the door. I'm freezing. I thought you were Helen."

"Sorry to disappoint you." He settled onto a slipcovered chair situated to her left.

"I'm not disappointed. I mean . . ." *Oops.*

He chuckled. "How're you doing?"

Nice. He let her out of the pickle she'd talked herself into. "Paint free—at least I hope I am." It had taken quite a lot of work to get it all out of her hair. Looked like he'd managed to escape getting paint on himself—at least she assumed he had. He smelled fresh, like he'd showered recently. "How'd everything go after I left? Did Derek get the floor cleaned?"

"For the most part. Helen took a look, and she didn't seem upset in the slightest. She was more concerned for you but decided to give you some space."

"Didn't stop you." She raised her chin.

"Nope. I don't mind making a pain out of myself." He winked.

She chuckled. "You're not a pain, Blake." He was the opposite. More like balm to soothe the rough edges of her day.

"I'm glad. Since you've arrived in Oak Knoll it seems all you've done is help me. I'd like to offer my services to you. What do *you* need besides an extra set of eyes?"

"Ha ha. I only fell because my mind was pre-occupied."

"I figured that had to be it." He leaned forward. "Maybe I can help. What's going on?"

Although not sure why, she knew she could trust

Blake. "There's nothing you can do, but it might help to talk about it. I know I've only been here a little more than a week, but something has come up at my restaurant that I must deal with in person."

He made himself comfortable as if planning to stay for a while. "What happened?"

"Jeff, my executive chef, gave his two-week notice. He received the opportunity of a lifetime at a place in New York."

"The guy who dumped you when you wouldn't marry him?" He blew out a long breath. "So he quit to get back at you?"

"Maybe. I don't know." She shrugged. "But I need to hire a replacement for him as soon as possible."

He sighed and looked down. "When will you leave?"

"I have someone working on it for me. Once she finds a chef, I'll fly home and interview the candidate to see if I agree with her choice. Hopefully, I will, and that will be the end of it, but if I don't, then I'll stick around until I find someone. When I opened Estelle's, I was the cook. I can do it again if necessary." Although her passion for her restaurant wasn't what it used to be and she hoped and prayed it wouldn't come to that.

He looked at her squarely. "Will you get back together with Jeff?"

"Not a chance. I don't love him like that. I should've broken up with him a long time ago, but I guess I was too comfortable and didn't want to mess up anything. He's a good guy." Heat rushed to her face. She sounded so shallow. Staying in a relationship simply so she didn't rock the boat was stupid, and in the process she had hurt Jeff. Guilt knotted her stomach. She glanced at Blake. "I'm sorry about the theater."

"What do you mean?"

"Well, I expect to miss more than a few rehearsals."

"I hadn't processed that far yet." Disappointment filled his eyes.

She didn't blame him. She'd taken on a lot with the children's theater, and for her to walk out now would be a challenge for him. At least he had a team of volunteers who could pick up the slack. But none of them would be able to be Kayla's understudy. She'd be breaking her word to both Kayla and Blake. That was what worried her the most about leaving.

~

"You named your restaurant Estelle's?" Blake's mind was playing catch-up with everything she'd just told him. The name struck him as unoriginal for such an original person. "Then again, I suppose your name is your brand." The ramifications of her words were finally sinking in. What would he do if Estelle had to be gone for an extended time?

"I know it sounds conceited, but you're right about my name being my brand, plus at the time it seemed like a good idea. You look like you might have a panic attack. It's going to be okay. I'm sure Amber will be a great help and—"

"Not Amber." She was nice and everything, but there were times she made him feel uncomfortable, as if she wanted him to ask her out. He wasn't interested in dating Amber—she wasn't his type. Okay, maybe she was, but he wasn't attracted to her like he was to Estelle.

He sucked in a hard breath. She hadn't showed the slightest bit of interest, which was probably for the best. She was fresh off a long-term relationship, and probably headed back to California sooner than later.

"What's wrong with Amber?" Concern filled her voice.

"Nothing." He shrugged and stood, walking to the fireplace and resting an elbow on the mantle, his focus on the flameless box below. "I don't know what to say." He barely got the words out.

He couldn't tell her where his thoughts had strayed. The realization that he had more than a passing interest in Estelle and the news that she would be leaving for an undetermined amount of time hit him to his core. He never should have allowed her into his life.

"O-kay . . ." She dragged out the word. "If you're worried about Amber, I can talk to her. Maybe you misunderstood her. She's kind of a touchy-feely person. I've seen her act like that with other people too. She probably doesn't even realize she's flirting."

"So you noticed too?"

She nodded. "I rescued you, remember?"

"Please don't say anything to her. If you're right,

she'll only get embarrassed, and she might quit. I can't lose both of you."

"You're not losing me. I only need some time away to get things straightened out. I'll be back." She shivered and ran her hands up and down her arms. "Does it always get so cold at the end of such a nice sunny day?"

"No." He pointed to a switch on the wall. "If you're cold, why not start a fire? It only takes the flip of the switch since it's gas."

Her mouth opened slightly. "That's okay." She set the computer on the coffee table and stood to face him. "Back to the subject. I won't say anything to Amber, but we need to make a plan so you aren't scrambling when I leave."

When not *if.* There was no hope then that she'd change her mind and try to manage things long distance. Disappointment hit him again. "What can I say to make you change your mind about leaving?"

Her face filled with regret. "There's nothing *to* say. I have to deal with this in person. I also need to clear the air with Jeff. I don't want him leaving for New York bitter and angry."

He was drawn to her all the more for her care and concern for this man. But at the same time, if she couldn't make something work with the chef of her own restaurant, what chance did he have, living in another state? He had to keep from feeling anything more for her. "What can I do to help?"

"Pray we find someone fast. This could drag on for

months."

"Months?" He was thinking a few weeks, not months.

Estelle nodded. "I'm so sorry." She stepped close to him and rested a hand on his arm. Her touch shot tingles through him. "If I had thought for even a minute that something like this would happen while I was here, I never would have become so involved with the theater."

Unshed tears shown in her eyes, twisting his gut. A breath of expectancy hung between them. He wanted to pull her close and tell her everything would be okay, but he refused to give in to the impulse.

She removed her hand from his arm and crossed her arms. "Maybe starting a fire would be a good idea after all." She flipped the switch, and heat burst from the gas-powered flames. She returned to her spot on the couch.

The hot flames forced him to move away. He parked himself in the chair again. "This musical will fall apart without you. I have a strong team of volunteers in place, but if you aren't Kayla's understudy, she'll quit. Those were her terms."

Disappointment filled her face. "I know, but I'm hoping she'll be reasonable when I explain the situation. Plus we still have two weeks before I'd absolutely have to leave. If we find someone before that, maybe I can fly the person here for the interview instead of going there."

His head snapped in her direction. "That's a great idea." *Lord please send someone fast. We need Estelle here.*

Her eyes lit. "It is, isn't it? It popped into my head

right as I said it."

He chuckled and flipped a throw pillow at her. "You're a nut, Estelle Rogers."

"Certifiable for sure," she deadpanned. She tossed the pillow back at him, catching him in the chin.

He relished the light moment. "This means war, lady."

Her blue eyes widened. She squealed and leapt over the back of the couch, taking cover. Her hand reached over the top and felt around, presumably for a pillow.

He held back a laugh. Instead he ducked down on all fours and nudged the pillow within her reach. Her slender fingers tugged it over the back of the couch. A second later she crouched and flung it at him hitting his head.

He tossed it back, missing her. He grabbed two more pillows, one in each hand and crept around to where she'd taken cover. "Ha." He raised the pillows.

She drew her knees to her chest, tucked her chin, and shielded her head with her arms. "I surrender. I surrender."

Laughing, he eased down beside her, stretching his legs out in front of him. He needed that—they both did.

She tilted her head and peeked at him then raised her head. A twinkle lit her eyes. "Thanks."

His insides turned to mush as he folded his hand around hers. "Anytime. I'm already praying you don't have to leave."

"Good. Me too." She angled her face in his

direction. "If anyone had told me a week ago we'd be sitting here like this, I never would've believed him."

"Me neither. But you've grown on me."

She laughed, yanked her hand away, and shoved him in the shoulder.

They both laughed a moment longer, then sobered.

"Blake?"

"Hmm?" Worry at her tone squeezed out the carefree feeling of a moment ago.

"You know there's a strong probability I'll have to leave, right? Everything might not work out the way we want."

He nodded. "I know," he said softly. The last thing he wanted was for Estelle to go, but he'd be grateful for any time he had with her. Not to mention the kids would be devastated.

8

Estelle sat with Kayla at the bar in Java World, looking out onto Main Street. "I realize what I told you is a shock," Estelle said, "but I hope you won't quit the musical because of me."

Kayla kept her focus on something beyond the window. "I have so many thoughts swirling around in my mind right now, I don't know where to begin. When I first found out who Derek really was, I was certain he'd leave Oak Knoll one day and return to his life as a pop music star. He assured me that wouldn't happen, but then it did."

"That's not entirely true, Kayla. He came back."

"I know. I'm going somewhere with this. At least I think I am." Kayla frowned. "I know he left with you for a valid reason, and I supported that decision. I also know your situation is valid. But I don't think I can do this without you. You are my security blanket."

"I understand, but you really don't need me. Rehearsals are going well, and by the time the performance weekend rolls around, you'll wonder why you ever thought you needed me."

Kayla looked at her with skepticism in her eyes. "That's doubtful. Something in me says you need to be here." Kayla twisted to face her. "I don't know why, but you can't leave. I need you. We all need you." She chuckled drily. "I never thought I'd say those words to *you*."

Estelle made a silly face. "Aw, come on. You know you love me." It was no secret they'd had a rocky start to their friendship, but then everything changed, and they'd been good friends ever since.

"Like a sister, my friend. But you make me want to scream in frustration."

"Don't do that. You might hurt your vocal chords."

Kayla sobered. "Good point. Please promise me you'll at least be here for the performances."

"Done. No matter what happens, I will be here that weekend. Besides, I'll have to come back for my car eventually."

"I'm going to hold you to that. If you aren't here, you'll have the wrath of the entire town to deal with."

"You do realize I'd be a thousand miles away?"

"Doesn't matter. I have connections." Kayla waggled her brows. "We'd better get to rehearsal."

"Thanks, Kayla."

"For what?"

"Not flipping out on me."

"Like I ever flip out." Kayla rolled her eyes.

Her friend had reason to be furious, but once again had chosen the high road. This was why they got along so well. Kayla was as true a friend as they came.

"I should go so I don't miss my call time." Kayla stood. "Are you coming to rehearsal?"

Estelle shook her head. "I'll be along in a little while." Blake needed to get used to her not being there. There was no better time than the present.

"Okay." Kayla gave her a quick hug. "I'll see you later."

"Yep." She waited for Kayla to leave then pulled out her phone. Her manager had sent her the résumé of a chef from Malibu. He specialized in fish dishes and fresh American cuisine. She'd never heard of him, but if his references panned out, she'd be willing to give him a try.

Gabby walked up to her. "How's it going, Estelle?"

Talk about a loaded question. "Okay. How are things?"

"There's a lull right now, but it'll pick up soon. I hear you're taking off."

Irritation rose up in her. "Who told you that?"

She shrugged. "Oh, you know. I pick up bits of conversations."

"Hmm." *Note to self; don't talk about anything confidential in Java World.* And here she thought their conversation had been private.

"It's too bad you have to go. I hear the moms talking about you when they're in here. They love that you're working with their kids."

"Really?" No one had said anything to her. Maybe an eavesdropping barista/business owner wasn't such a bad thing after all. "I enjoy my time at the theater."

"So you have an opening at your restaurant?"

"Does everyone know my business?" Her voice sounded huffy to her own ears, but she didn't care.

"The reason I bring it up is because I have a cousin who is a fabulous cook."

"He's welcome to submit his resume to Jamie, the manager at Estelle's in Costa Mesa."

"He is a she, and I'll let her know." She tucked a stray strand of hair behind her ear. "I need to get back to work. Would you like another tea? On the house."

"Thanks, but I'm good."

Gabby nodded and headed to the kitchen.

Estelle ought to have told her that she had a candidate in mind already, so her cousin wouldn't get her hopes up, but if this guy didn't work out, she'd need to keep looking. She shot off several emails inquiring about the chef Jamie had selected. It would be great if this one turned out to be a keeper, but she knew better than to get overly excited.

Estelle gathered her stuff then headed toward the door. "Have a good one, Gabby."

"Thanks. You too."

She waved and left the coffee hangout. She was officially an hour late to rehearsal. She'd warned Blake about it being a possibility. Hopefully everything had gone smoothly, and he hadn't stressed about her not showing.

She strolled up the street. A couple of people she'd never seen before said hi, but thankfully kept walking. What was it with this town? Everyone was so nice.

The community center came into view. She dodged a couple of kids as they charged out with their mother chasing after them. Estelle chuckled, thankful she wasn't that woman. She walked inside and went directly to the auditorium.

Piano music greeted her as she stepped in. But complete chaos ruled the stage. What was going on?

~

Blake ground his teeth for the umpteenth time in the past hour. What had happened to everyone? It was like they'd forgotten what they'd learned last week. Maybe he shouldn't have announced that Estelle wouldn't be staying for the entire summer. But he'd had to say something since the entire cast had been whispering about where she might be when she didn't show up for rehearsal this morning.

A shrill whistle sounded above the chaos. He shielded his eyes and looked toward the seats. *Estelle?* He couldn't help but be impressed. The woman could whistle.

"What's going on in here?" Estelle marched up to the stage with her hands planted on her waist. "I recognize the song, but whatever you call what you were doing was not what we rehearsed last week."

A murmur broke out amongst the kids. One little girl started crying.

Estelle stepped over to her and squatted to her level. "What are the tears about?"

"You yelled at us. And you're leaving." Her bottom lip puckered.

Estelle's brow furrowed. She hugged the little girl, then rose and faced everyone. "I see you heard about my predicament. I want to assure all of you that I will be here often and for as long as I am able. I had something I needed to deal with this morning, and that's why I'm late, but that's no excuse for what I walked in on. You are all so much better than that."

Ten sets of wide eyes were trained on Estelle. She definitely knew how to hold the attention of these kids. Blake held his breath—this could either go very well, or very bad. What if they all quit? He almost laughed at the thought. These kids were here because they loved it. They weren't going anywhere.

"Now let's start from the top, and this time I want to see what you're capable of." She counted off the beats, and the piano player began the opening song. Estelle moved off the stage and sat in the front row.

Blake eased down the stairs and sank into the chair beside hers. "That was . . . impressive." He kept his voice low.

"What happened?" she asked while keeping her focus on the kids.

"They were out of sorts when you didn't show up on time. I thought it would be best to be honest with them, but it made everything worse. They were distracted and couldn't seem to remember anything they'd learned."

"So I saw. Somehow we've got to get them to realize they don't need me here. How did you get their best in past years?" She looked his way but quickly pulled her focus back to the stage.

"I don't know. For starters there were fewer kids and the musicals have been simpler." In past years they didn't have a movie star at rehearsals that they were trying to impress—or the disappointment when said movie star didn't live up to their expectations.

The song ended. Estelle stood. "Better. Amber, I leave them in your capable hands." She turned to Blake. "A word?" She motioned toward the side exit.

Uh-oh. He had the distinct feeling he was about to be chewed out. How was it that Estelle could come in here and think she could take over? Then again, he'd let her. The door closed behind them. "Look. I appreciate that you got them back on track, but I'm the director, and I'd thank you to let me do my job."

Surprise lit her face then her eyes narrowed. "Then do your job." She glared.

How could a person's eyes spark with such emotion? "I was, until you interrupted."

"Seriously?"

He rubbed the back of his neck. Getting defensive

wouldn't serve any good purpose. "What did you want?"

She scrunched her face. "I forgot." Her face pinked and became blotchy. "Oh. I remember now. I have a potential chef. If his references are good, I'll either fly him here or fly home for the weekend. I shouldn't miss any rehearsals if this guy works out."

He almost did a fist pump but stopped himself just in time. "That's great." Relief filled him. "I thought you brought me here to chew me out."

"Why would I do that? I know this situation isn't easy for anyone. My hope is to make it as painless as possible."

Remorse hit him for the way he'd acted. "About what I said. I'm sorry for jumping on your case. I could have handled things better with you and with the kids."

"We agree on that at least." She shot him a cheeky grin.

"So you think this chef is the one?"

"I hope so, but it's too soon to say for certain. Don't worry, Blake. I'll be sure to talk to the kids before they leave today about my expectations for them when I'm not here. Hopefully that will make a difference." A grin tugged at her lips. "Maybe I'll tell them you'll be recording rehearsals to show me, so they'd better do their best."

"Now that's a great idea!" Too bad he hadn't thought of it sooner. The kids loved to watch their performances. "I'm going to start recording today. That way they can see what they need to work on. Then at the end of the summer I'll give them each a before and after file."

"Nice." She nodded toward the door that led to the auditorium. "Shall we?"

He'd rather stand here with her all to himself, but duty called. He strode behind Estelle. Amber had the children well in hand. *Whew.* Maybe this morning would be an isolated incident.

Estelle's phone buzzed. She checked the caller ID. "I have to take this. Sorry." She lowered her voice. "Hi, Jamie. You did. Oh. That's unfortunate." Her shoulders sagged.

Blake couldn't help listening to the one-sided conversation. Clearly it was about the potential chef, and it didn't sound good. In fact, Estelle looked rather defeated.

"Okay. Send me your number two choice after you check his references this time. 'Bye." She pocketed her phone and looked to Blake. "Good thing we checked references. That chef I was hoping to hire was fired from his last job for sexual harassment."

He winced. "Now what?"

"We move on. There were several applicants." She raised her chin and focused forward.

Pride swelled in him. Estelle was something. She didn't cave when things didn't go her way. The opposite, in fact—she seemed to grow more determined and perhaps stronger.

The remainder of rehearsal went well, including

Estelle's speech about recording them. They seemed excited about the idea. Hopefully that would translate into a stronger performance in the end.

An hour later Blake and Estelle walked outside together. He had a million and one things to do but he didn't want his time with Estelle to end. "You want to grab lunch with me?"

"I could eat. Helen keeps talking about a place called Deli on the Rye."

"I know the place." He suspected the reason Helen talked about the deli all the time was because she had a crush on Nick, the owner. The funny thing was, Nick seemed to like her too, but neither was aware of the other's interest.

"Great. Lead the way." She wove her arm through his. "Considering everything, I think today went fabulous."

He warmed at her touch and struggled to focus. "Agreed. Hopefully, they'll continue their momentum. How did it go with Kayla this morning?"

"Not great, but okay. I doubt she'll quit, so don't stress that. We need to make sure she feels more than capable of pulling off her role."

"She's plenty capable," Blake said.

"*I* can see that and so can you, but it's going to take some time to convince her."

He nodded. "Here we are." He pulled open the deli's door. The scent of freshly baked bread whooshed over them.

"Mmm. If the food tastes as good as it smells, I understand why it's a favorite of Helen's. I think I'll try one of the specials."

They placed their orders then searched for a seat amongst the bustling lunch crowd. Maybe coming here wasn't his best idea. They'd have to practically shout to be heard over the roar of this place. He guided them to a corner table. At least they were off by themselves a little. He sat with his back to the wall.

Estelle looked around. "This is the place to be. I didn't expect business to be so brisk."

"We don't have a lot of choices in Oak Knoll for lunch. There's the diner, a pizza place, Java World, a food truck that parks on the edge of town, and then here."

"Sounds to me like a good market to open something new."

"You thinking of expanding?"

"I wasn't, but you never know."

A teenage boy brought them their sandwiches nestled on wax paper in a plastic basket. Blake prayed a blessing for their food then raised the roast beef on rye to his mouth. He breathed in deeply of the scent of the bread. There was nothing else like it.

Estelle's eyes twinkled as she watched him enjoy his meal.

"What?"

She raised her brows and shook her head. "Nothing."

He nodded toward her untouched turkey breast sandwich on whole wheat. "You're not eating."

"I was having fun watching you enjoy your sandwich." She shrugged, picked up a half and took a delicate bite.

He chuckled. "Trust me, Nick makes the best sandwiches. You don't have to be afraid."

She swallowed. "I'm not afraid. Just cautious. You're right, it's good. Not sure it's the *best* I've ever had, but close."

"And here I thought mine were the best," a male voice said.

"Nick!" Blake said. How had the man snuck up on them without him noticing? "Have you met Estelle?"

"Her reputation precedes her, but not that I recall." Nick offered a hand to her. "It's a pleasure to meet you. Rumor has it you're looking for a new chef at your restaurant in California. I wanted to put in a good word for Gabby's cousin Cerise. She worked here for a short time right after culinary school. The lady knows how to run a kitchen, and she has good ideas."

Blake watched Estelle's face closely, wondering how she'd feel about the small town information network. Whatever she was thinking, she hid it well.

"Thanks, Nick. No decision has been made yet, but please make sure she sends her résumé to Estelle's in Costa Mesa. My manager and I will be hiring someone very soon."

"I'm sure she's on top of that." He clapped a hand

on Blake's shoulder. "Good to see you. Tell Helen hi for me."

"Will do. Or you could tell her yourself. She's always at the farm. Why not stop in sometime?"

Surprise lit Nick's face. "I couldn't do that." He sauntered away.

"He seems like a nice man," Estelle said.

"He is."

She frowned. "But I can't figure out how he knew about my conversation with Gabby. They both own their own place. How would either of them have time to step out and talk?"

"You've heard of a smart phone?"

She made a face. "Duh. She texted him. Don't ask why I thought they'd do things differently here simply because it's a small town." She took another bite of her sandwich. "This is good, but I should have asked for avocado. That would've put it over the top."

He teasingly rolled his eyes. Talk about a foodie. "Are you actually going to consider Gabby's cousin?" He couldn't imagine her hiring someone who wasn't well known, but she'd proven him wrong time and again, so anything was possible when it came to Estelle.

"I'll make sure her résumé is looked at. Beyond that, no promises. Her references would need to be mind blowing considering the caliber of chefs she's up against for this position."

He figured as much.

"Do you know Gabby's cousin?" Estelle asked.

"No. I didn't even know she had one until Nick brought her up. That being said, Nick doesn't hand out compliments or recommendations freely."

"Good to know."

They finished eating in silence. He nodded to her basket; it still held a pickle slice. "You going to eat that?"

She slid it over toward him. "Help yourself."

"Don't mind if I do." Nick made his own pickles, and no one with any sense left them in the basket. Blake bit into the spear and savored the juices. "You have no idea what you're missing. These are homemade."

"I never acquired a taste for them."

"Your loss." He tossed the other half into his mouth then stood. "I need to get back to the community center. I'm meeting with the volunteers."

Estelle followed his lead. "Why wasn't I included?"

"I figured since you're leaving, there was no point in dragging you to a meeting."

She shot a look of annoyance at him. "It would have been nice to be given the choice. As long as I'm here, I don't want to miss anything."

He raised both hands. "Okay, okay—I won't make that mistake again."

Her face relaxed. "Thank you."

He hadn't realized this musical was so important to her. His heart warmed at her passion for his pet project.

A commotion on the sidewalk outside drew his attention.

9

Estelle rose on tiptoe, hoping to see what had drawn the crowd's attention. Was someone injured? She didn't hear any sirens and no emergency responders were parked nearby. She turned to Blake. "Can you see what the problem is?"

A grim look covered his face. "Come on. We need to take the back exit." He gripped her forearm and tugged her toward the kitchen.

If she didn't trust Blake, there was no way she'd allow him to forcefully direct her like this. "What's wrong?" Her pulse amped.

"Nick, Estelle needs to duck out the back way. Okay?"

"No problem." Nick tugged off his apron and went in the direction they'd come.

She needed to take the back exit? She dug in her feet and refused to move. "Hold on. Why do *I* need to leave this way? What did you see out there?"

"I recognized a photographer. He's rather

aggressive, and I figured you'd prefer to avoid the paparazzi, but if I was wrong . . ." He removed his hand from her arm. "By all means, take the front exit."

Estelle's pulse thrummed in her ears. "How did you know he's a paparazzo?" Did Blake tip him off that she was here working on his musical to drum up interest in his work? She crossed her arms and focused on his face.

He didn't so much as blink. "Trinity and I were at one of Derek's concerts years ago. There was one man in particular who was very aggressive. He got into a scuffle with one of the guys on Derek's security team."

"Oh." She remembered that. Derek had been pretty upset, and it wasn't long after that he took off for Italy and then settled here to be with his mom. "I'm sorry for thinking you had anything to do with him being here."

But how did the media know she was here? Maybe he wasn't here for her at all. Then again, maybe he had found out about the musical. Panic filled her. What should she do? It wasn't like she could hide from him forever. If he knew about the musical, then he'd simply lie in wait at the community center. No, it was best to face this head on—even if he was an unpleasant person.

"What are you thinking?" Blake narrowed his eyes as he studied her.

"That some things, or rather people, need to be dealt with and not ignored. In this case Mr. Paparazzo. The sooner I give him the photo op and sound bite he wants, the sooner we can be rid of him." She tugged on his arm.

He didn't budge. "Are you sure about this?"

"No, but I'm going with it anyway. Come on. I want you with me." The paparazzi scared her. Always had. They were a necessary evil once upon a time, but no more. She glanced over her shoulder as they exited the kitchen. "Stay close."

"I'm here."

As she pushed out the door, an unexpected calmness filled her. She squared her shoulders and plastered on her camera-ready smile.

The crowd parted and hushed. It looked like he'd been interviewing the community. Had he turned into a reporter or something?

He looked in her direction and smiled. "Ms. Rogers. Just the woman I wanted to talk to."

The crowd's attention turned to her.

"I'm walking to the community center. We can talk on the way."

His eyes widened. "Works for me." He shouldered his camera bag on one side and held a voice recorder in the other. His camera was draped around his neck. No telephoto lens—interesting. That used to be a staple of this particular man.

She set out toward the community center with Blake to her right and the "reporter" to her left. A plethora of questions swam around in her mind, but she refused to speak until spoken to. There was no reason she needed to make his job easier.

"Word is that *Estelle's* is going under. Do you care to

comment?" He thrust the voice recorder in her face.

Estelle's? That's why he was here? She took a breath and let it out in a puff. "I have no idea what you're talking about. Estelle's doors will not be closing anytime in the foreseeable future."

"According to my sources, your chef quit and most of your kitchen staff did as well."

Panic shot through her. Could he be right? Had Jamie kept the full truth from her? "Who is your source?"

"A good reporter never reveals his sources."

"You're suggesting you're a good reporter? That's rich."

Blake cleared his throat and rested a hand on her back.

"Tell you what, you tell me your source, and I'll give you an interview. Until that time we're done." She walked up the steps to the community center.

"What are you doing in Oak Knoll? The townspeople said you were volunteering with the children's theater. Why are you here when your restaurant is falling apart, Ms. Rogers?"

She let him shoot questions at her back, never once altering her gait.

Blake opened the door. "After you."

"Thanks." Her voice barely above a whisper. "Do you mind if I use your office? I need to make a private phone call."

"Not at all. Should I hold the meeting for you?"

She shook her head. "I don't know how long this will take."

Concern filled his face. "Do you think he was telling the truth?"

"That's what I aim to find out. There's no reason for him to make it up. I've been off his radar for years. I can't imagine why I am suddenly news, unless there's more going on than I'm aware of. Regardless of how this phone conversation goes, I'll be on the next flight out of Portland. I need to see with my own eyes what's going on."

His shoulders drooped slightly. "I understand. You do what you must. We'll be here when you get back."

"Thanks for understanding." Blake was a true friend. She appreciated that he didn't lay a guilt trip on her. She hustled to his office backstage and closed the door. The meeting would more than likely be in the auditorium, so no one would be nearby to overhear.

She called Jamie's cell phone.

After four rings, Jamie picked up. "Before you say anything, it wasn't me. I'd hoped to contain the story, but failed. I assume that's why you're calling."

"So it's true?" Estelle slumped against the chair back.

"Half the kitchen staff is moving to New York with Jeff. I had hoped to rehire help quickly, but there's more."

Estelle closed her eyes, bracing herself for whatever Jamie had to tell her.

"Someone has been stealing from the till. I don't know who, and until I can narrow it down, I don't want to hire anyone new."

"Great. Just great." She leaned forward and rested her head in her hands. "I'll be there tomorrow. Don't do or say anything to anyone."

"But the media wants to know what's going on."

"And how do they know about any of this?"

"Well, it seems someone here tipped them off."

"Who?"

"I may have said something to my sister."

"Jamie!" Her sister was a reporter with a local TV station. "Of all people. Why?"

"I needed advice. I didn't think about her being a reporter. She's my sister."

Estelle took a long, slow breath, stopping herself before she fired her manager and was left with no one to run the restaurant in her absence. "I trusted you."

"I know. And I'm sorry."

"Keep things together until I get there. Can you do that for me?" If someone had told her she'd doubt Jamie's competence and loyalty even a week ago, she'd have stuck up for the woman. How had things gone bad so fast?

"I'll do my best, Estelle."

Estelle hung up and left the office. She sent her assistant a text to book her on an evening flight out of PDX.

Blake parted the black velvet-like curtains and

stopped when he saw her. "You look like you lost your best friend."

"Pretty close. I have to pack. My assistant is booking me on a flight for tonight. Things are a lot worse than I knew. I'm sorry, Blake, but I don't know if I'll be back before the performances."

"It's okay. I understand. We've got this. Don't worry." He rested a hand on her shoulder. "Everything will work out."

How could he be so sweet when she was bailing on him? She blinked back tears then wrapped her arms around his middle and held tight.

His body slowly relaxed as he held her. "I'll be praying for you."

The tension lifted, and she breathed easier. When was the last time someone had that effect on her? She tilted her head back. "Thanks. I'll call you when I know more." She stepped out of his embrace.

He gave her hand a gentle squeeze and looked into her eyes. "If you need anything, I'm only a phone call away."

"And a thousand miles."

He waved away her concern. "It's only a two hour flight or a day's drive. No biggie."

She gave him a sad smile. "Thank you, Blake. I'd better get a move on."

"Do you need a ride to the airport?"

She bit down on her bottom lip. "I forgot about that. I don't want to leave my car there indefinitely."

Amber stepped from the other side of the curtains. "I love going to PDX. I'd be happy to take you, Estelle."

"You were eavesdropping?" Blake asked.

"Not really. I was heading back here to ask you a question when I overhead you ask Estelle about needing a ride."

"I'll take you up on that, Amber. Thanks. When I know my itinerary I'll text it to you." She'd rather Blake took her but it would be easier this way.

Three hours later, Estelle sat beside Amber in her Honda sedan. "I sure appreciate you taking me to the airport. Especially during this time of day. The traffic is a pain."

"I like driving, and I love going to Portland, so you're doing me a favor by giving me a reason to go there."

They drove in silence, listening to the radio for close to an hour when Amber glanced toward Estelle. "So is there anything going on between you and Blake?"

Estelle thought of their hug, but that had probably meant nothing to him. "No. But I thought you had your sights on him."

"What?" She glanced toward Estelle. "No way."

"You were flirting with him at the barn the other day." Estelle watched Amber closely, and then it hit her—she'd promised not to say anything about the flirting. Big oops. But she couldn't take it back now.

"I was? How embarrassing. I've been told I'm a flirt, but I don't mean to be. I tend to be too friendly, and it's misunderstood as flirting." She shook her head. "How will I ever face him again?"

Estelle could tell the woman was being truthful, and she felt for her. "Don't worry about it. I'm sure he's forgotten all about it. But out of curiosity, why aren't you interested in him? He's single, good looking, solid as a rock, sweet . . ." Estelle's face heated. Great—she'd better not get all blotchy again.

Amber shot her a knowing look. "I suppose he's all those things, but he comes with way too much baggage."

Estelle twisted to face Amber. "You're kidding."

"No. Why would I kid about that? You know about his wife and daughter? He blames himself that they died. That's a big burden to carry alone—baggage."

Estelle frowned and faced forward. Her gaze locked on the truck in front of them. She knew about Trinity and Kendal, but why did he blame himself? Surely he didn't think a car accident he had nothing to do with was his fault. Sadness that he carried that burden settled on her. "Okay, so you're not into men with baggage no matter how ruggedly handsome?"

"Nope. He's all yours, and if I'm reading him right, he's interested too."

Estelle's head whipped toward the driver's side of the car. Had Amber also seen their hug and read too much into it? She had to explain. "Blake could barely stand me when we first met. There's no way he's interested. Granted he's a great friend, but beyond that . . ." She shook her head. Could Amber be right? She

119

caught her breath. What was wrong with her? She'd just broken one man's heart, and here she was excited by the possibility that Blake was attracted to her.

Amber shrugged. "I suppose I don't know him all that well. My aunt told me what I know, so maybe I read him wrong. He's a pretty serious guy. I try to lighten things up when I'm around him, but . . . well." Amber sighed and flipped on her blinker as she took the exit to Airport Road.

Estelle chuckled. That explained so much. "As soon as I get things straightened out with my restaurant I'll be back. Maybe I'll help you try to lighten him up."

Amber smiled. "That could be fun. Give me a heads up, and I'll come get you."

"How is it you have time? Don't you have a dance studio to run?"

"My studio is still small, and most of my classes are on Saturdays. Thanks to the students I've been picking up from the theater, I might be able to add another class to my schedule soon, but I still have plenty of time to come and get you." She moved over to the drop-off lane and braked. "Here you go."

"Thanks again." Estelle hopped out and grabbed her bags from the backseat. "See you."

"'Bye." Amber waved and pulled into traffic.

What an interesting person. Estelle looked forward to getting to know her. But right now she had to get checked in and through security.

~

Blake sat in his room in the barn, staring at the wall. He could move back to the cottage but hoped Estelle would return sooner than later. Weariness weighed on him. He missed her already, and she'd only been gone two days. Rehearsals had gone well—much better than he'd expected, considering Estelle's sudden departure. It still amazed him how easily the kids had bonded with her.

A knock sounded on his door.

"Come in." He sat up.

"There you are," Helen said. "I've been looking all over for you. I saw your pickup, but you weren't in the cottage."

"No. I decided to stay here for a while."

"I see. You're hoping Estelle will be back." Helen stepped over to the lone chair in the room. "Do you mind if I sit?"

"Not at all. What's on your mind?"

"More like who. It's not the same around here without Estelle. I know she was only here a short time, but she fit in like she belonged."

Dare he admit out loud that he missed her? "Maybe you should go visit your granddaughters. That'll tire you out enough you won't have the energy to miss anyone."

"I'm already ahead of you. They're spending the morning with me tomorrow. Derek can't watch them during rehearsal."

Blake nodded. "Have you heard from Estelle?"

She pressed her lips tight and shook her head once. "I hope things at her restaurant weren't as bad as she feared."

"Me too." He wanted her to return to Oak Knoll. He felt something with her he hadn't felt in a long time. "I was hoping she'd communicated with you."

"Not yet. Before she came for a visit we would exchange emails a couple of times a week."

"I had no idea." Helen and Estelle were much closer than he'd realized.

"I haven't seen you this down since you first came to Oak Knoll."

He jerked his head back. "I'm sure I'm not that bad." Was he really that low over a woman he'd only met a short time ago? There was no way Estelle's leaving compared to the loss of his wife and daughter. Then again, he hadn't come here until a year after their deaths.

"You could always Facetime or Skype with her."

He raised a brow. "Listen to you. I had no idea you were up on that kind of stuff."

She shrugged. "Derek and Kayla taught me so I could visit with the girls while they're traveling."

That sounded like his buddy. Family was everything to Derek. "I don't think Estelle would appreciate me trying to Facetime her, but maybe a text to see how things are going would be okay."

Helen nodded. "Of course it would be okay."

He cleared his throat. "Nick asked about you the other day. He said to say hello."

Her eyes lit. "Really? That was nice of him." She was quiet for a moment, clearly thinking. "I've been keeping busy in the garden, but I could use a day off to run errands. Maybe I'll stop in there tomorrow." She strode toward the door.

"Good idea. You deserve to find some happiness."

She stopped and faced him. A frown puckered her brow. "What is *that* supposed to mean?"

Uh-oh. "Only that you've been alone for a long time. Maybe you and Nick would be good for each other." Oh boy—that did not come out the way he wanted it to. *What happened to staying out of it?* His head was more messed up than he'd realized.

"I love you like a son, Blake, but you have no idea what you're talking about. I am plenty happy."

"Sure, but I think Nick likes you, and I thought—"

She raised a hand, silencing him. "Stop right there. I won't listen to another word. Have a good evening." She pivoted and marched out.

"Great," he muttered under his breath. Should he go after her? No, he'd only make it worse with the state of his mind. He pulled out his cell phone and opened his texting app. "How are things? Concerned about you. Call or text with an update soon. Blake." He added his name in case she hadn't programed his number into her phone. His thumb hovered over the send button. He pressed it before he chickened out. There was no reason he couldn't text her. After all, they were friends.

His phone rang. Without thinking to look at the

screen he accepted the call. "Hello?"

"You said to call."

Pleasure coursed through him. "Estelle? I didn't expect to hear from you so quickly."

"You caught me at a good time. I'm between interviews."

"How's it going?" It was nice to hear her voice.

"Although it was bad when I got here, things weren't as bad as I was led to believe. I still don't know who has been stealing from me. I know I've only been here a couple of days, but I'd hoped to solve that mystery fast."

He frowned. Someone had been stealing too? "I'm sorry to hear that. At least you have a little good news."

"Yeah. I hate to say it, but I'm thankful the paparazzi tracked me down. Jamie was going to try to deal with all of this on her own. I suppose that's her job, but my name is on this place and well . . . you know?"

"Sure. Have you found a strong candidate for your chef?"

"Actually, you're not going to believe this, but I ended up hiring Gabby's cousin. As it turns out, I was already familiar with her. Small world."

"No kidding. So you like her then?"

"I do. She has the necessary experience. She isn't cocky, and she runs a great kitchen according to her references. I threw her into the kitchen last night with Jeff. That probably wasn't my best decision, but it went surprisingly well, and I was able to see her potential.

She's actually helping with the interviews as I work to build up the kitchen staff again."

Excitement filled him. "Great. So when will you be back?"

"I'm sorry, Blake—the next interviewee is here. I have to go."

"All right. We can talk later." With a sigh he tossed his phone onto the bed next to him. At least she'd called. But had she deliberately evaded his question, or did she actually need to hang up?

10

Estelle looked around the empty dining room of her restaurant. She should have known Blake would want to know when she'd return to Oak Knoll. The truth was, things here weren't as great as she'd made them out to sound, but she didn't want him to worry or stress about her extended absence, so she'd downplayed her situation to him.

She had hurt Jeff far more than she'd realized. He did his best to avoid her, and it was clear she was the reason he had taken the job in New York. They had a divided workplace. Those staying supported her, and those leaving supported him. The whole thing made her sad. She still didn't know how to make things right with Jeff. Maybe only time could do that. As for everyone else, there was nothing she could do. She hadn't asked for them to choose a side.

Cerise couldn't start when Estelle needed her, so she had come up with a Plan B. Maybe she should have hired someone else, but she liked Cerise, and the woman's references were so amazing she would have been crazy to pass her up—plus she liked the idea of a female managing the kitchen. The only thing that bothered her was that no one had snagged Cerise sooner. Was there something she didn't know about Cerise? Then again, maybe her new cook had been particular about where she applied since her current gig was pretty good.

Cerise breezed into the dining room wearing capris, a flowing blouse, and flip-flops, while carrying two tall iced teas. "I forgot how tiring talking was." Her last word came out in a croak.

Estelle laughed. "To think I used to do it for a living. You should probably give your voice a rest. It sounds worn out."

She nodded and took a long draw from the straw in her drink. She leaned against the chair back and closed her eyes.

"Shall we hammer out who you want in your kitchen?" Estelle asked.

Cerise's eyelids opened slowly. "I suppose that would be a good idea." She reached for the résumés. "No." She slid one to the left, then another two. "Yes." She slid it to the right. This went on for several minutes as she pored over the applicants. Since over half of the kitchen staff had turned in their two-week's notices, there were several spots to fill.

Estelle leafed through the small stack Cerise had made. "You'd take any of these?" They didn't need all of them, and more than likely at least one would decline her offer. It seemed there was always one person who changed their mind after the interview.

"Yes. If their references are good, then whoever you liked best will be fine with me."

"Good. Is there anyone in particular you'd be disappointed to not have in the kitchen?"

Cerise seemed to think for a moment then shook her head. "No."

"Okay then." Estelle offered her hand. "I'm looking forward to working with you. And if anything changes in your timeline, allowing you to get here sooner, please let me know."

Cerise grasped her hand in a firm shake then released it. "I will."

"Thanks. I do have one more question that's been bugging me."

Cerise raised a brow. "Oh? What's that?"

"Why hasn't anyone snatched you up before me?" Estelle should have asked this question from the start. She prayed the reason was something she could live with.

"I hadn't found the right fit. The idea of personally hiring most of the kitchen staff was a huge draw for me."

"But how did you know about that?"

Cerise shrugged. "News travels."

"I guess so." Apparently it wasn't only small towns that could spread information like a wildfire.

"I should head out. See you in a couple weeks."

Estelle nodded. "Or sooner." She knew the chances Cerise could start earlier were slim, but also wanted the woman to know she was needed ASAP.

Cerise left via the front entrance.

A few minutes later the door opened again, and Jeff pulled up short. "Oh. I didn't realize you were here. I uh . . ." He looked around like he wanted to escape but didn't know where to go.

Estelle stood. "Actually, I'm glad you're here. Since we have the place to ourselves, do you think we could talk?"

His dark, brooding eyes latched onto hers. "I don't think we have anything to talk about."

Her chest tightened. He wasn't going to make this easy. "Maybe not, but I have something to say."

He ran a hand along the back of his neck, looking like he'd rather be anywhere but here. "Fine." He glowered.

She motioned toward a chair. "Maybe we could sit."

"Whatever." He sat where Cerise had been.

She eased down and rested her folded hands on the table.

"I've already sold my home and signed a contract with the restaurant in New York," he said "so you can't talk me out of going."

Her eyes widened. "Congratulations on selling your house so quickly. But that's not what I want to talk about. I need to apologize. You were right. I don't love you—at least not the way I should if I was going to marry you."

"Seriously? This is what you want to say to me?" He

leaned forward and started to stand.

"Please hear me out. This is important."

He sighed and planted himself back onto the seat. "Fine, but make it fast. I have work to do."

Her insides filled with butterflies. She took a breath and let it out slowly. "I need to apologize for hurting you. I never should have stayed in a relationship when we weren't both on the same page. I'm sorry. I knew you wanted to get married, and I didn't."

His gaze locked onto hers. "Ever?"

She ducked her chin. "Maybe not *ever*, but you and I lacked the passion a couple should have. We were like a comfortable pair of jeans. There was no spark."

"I like my old jeans. They're soft, and I always know what to expect when I put them on."

She agreed, but she wanted more. "Don't you want a little excitement? Something less predictable? Passion?"

"I never thought about it." He rubbed his chin as if considering her words.

Hope filled her. Maybe they could part on good terms after all. "I do love you, Jeff, but as a friend. I didn't realize it until you asked me to marry you. I'm so sorry. I hope you find true love in New York."

"I appreciate that." He blinked watery eyes and cleared his throat. "What about you?"

"Me?" Panic seized her. She had no idea what he wanted from her.

"Yeah. There's something different about you since you returned from Oregon."

She chuckled nervously. "I'm surprised you noticed." Considering he'd avoided her at every turn.

"I notice everything. You seem happier somehow, in spite of all that's going on here. Why?"

"I don't know. I didn't realize I was happier. I suppose working with the children's theater could be why. Acting is my first love. I didn't know how much I missed it." But could there be more to it than the theater? Blake's face flashed in her mind.

Jeff nodded. "I always knew you'd go back to acting one day. I thought being a restaurant owner was a passing hobby. To be honest, I expected you to go back to it sooner."

She tilted her head. "You never said anything." He really would make some woman happy one day. He was quite a catch—just not the catch for her.

"I didn't want to push you. I figured you'd find your way back when you were ready. When you told me you were thinking about visiting your friend in Oregon for the summer, I panicked. I knew you weren't ready to commit for a lifetime. I never should have asked—"

"Don't you dare apologize for proposing to me." She crossed her arms and gave him her I'm not messing around look.

He chuckled, then sobered. "Okay. I won't." He stood and opened his arms to her.

Estelle moved into his embrace and relaxed in his arms. "I'm going to miss this."

He rested his chin on the top of her head. "Not as

much as I will."

Why did he have to be so sweet? Her throat thickened, and she blinked away sudden tears. She stepped out of his arms. "So how do we move forward? The kids have taken sides."

He rubbed his chin. "Yeah, my staff is a loyal bunch. Except those who took your side." He was quiet for a minute. "I'll tell you what. Let's show them that we're friends. Maybe seeing us together again will heal the rift in the kitchen. I could use a night not filled with emotional tension."

That made two of them. "Deal. You're one of a kind, Jeff. I'm going to miss you."

He reached out and caressed her cheek. "Same."

"Hello?"

They both turned toward the door where Jamie gawked at them with wide eyes and an open mouth.

"Does this mean you're not leaving, Jeff?"

"Nope." He strolled to the kitchen.

Jamie rushed to her side. "What is going on between the two of you? I thought for sure he was going to kiss you."

Estelle frowned. "No." She glanced toward the kitchen, and for the first time since she'd come home, she felt truly happy. *Thank you, Lord.* She'd prayed for an opportunity to clear the air with Jeff, to give them both some hope for a cordial future. She couldn't have asked for a better outcome.

~

A week later Estelle came to a big decision after witnessing something she had never expected—Jamie skimming money from the till. Estelle could not leave her restaurant in Jamie's hands any longer. After closing, when everyone else had left, she called her manager into the kitchen.

"What's up?" Jamie asked. "I was on my way out."

The irony of the words struck Estelle as sad. She pressed her lips together and slowly untied her apron then hung it on a hook beside the door. "I'll be right back." She went to her office, opened the safe, and then pulled out an envelope.

"What are you doing?" Jamie asked from the doorway.

"I need your key." She held out her hand, palm up.

"Okay." Jamie pulled it off her key ring and handed it over. "Are you having the locks changed since Jeff left?"

"I'm firing you."

Jamie's mouth opened.

"Don't say anything you'll regret." Estelle held out the envelope. "Your final check minus the money you stole is inside."

"I didn't steal anything." Jamie crossed her arms with a defiant look on her face.

Estelle raised a brow and sighed. "I have you on video. You're lucky I'm not pressing charges. Take the check, and don't bother using me as a reference."

Jamie uncrossed her arms and looked ready to cry. "I can explain."

Estelle felt for the woman, but there was no way she would knowingly employ someone who stole from her. "I'm not interested in hearing your excuse. Please make sure you take all of your belongings with you as you leave."

"The tabloids were right about you." Jamie grabbed the check. "This stinks."

"I agree. You need to leave now." Estelle raised her chin high, refusing to give in to the hurt Jamie's words had caused. She had worked hard to change her reputation.

Jamie called her a few choice names then stormed from the restaurant.

With shaking hands, Estelle locked up the place then went to her office. She pulled out her cell phone and without thinking called Blake.

"Hello?" His voice sounded half asleep.

Relief flooded her, and her throat suddenly clogged with tears. "Hi, it's me."

"Estelle?" He sounded more awake now. "What's wrong?"

"I fired my manager tonight, and it didn't go well."

He let out a breath. "You okay?"

"I've been better." She cleared her throat and pulled herself together. "I just wanted to hear a friendly voice."

"Where are you?"

"At my restaurant." But she wished she were back in Oak Knoll where life wasn't so cruel. "I should probably head home, and let you go back to sleep."

"I don't need sleep. We can talk all night if you need to."

She chuckled and felt her shoulders relax. Calling Blake had been the right thing to do. "That's sweet, but I happen to know what a bear you are when you don't get enough rest. Thanks for answering the phone. Good night, Blake. I'll call you again soon."

~

"Five. Six. Seven. Eight." Amber clapped out the beats.

She had the kids well in hand as Blake pocketed his car keys and headed for the exit. Estelle was returning today. The past four weeks without her had been a drag, but ever since that night she'd fired her manager, she'd called him daily. They'd talked for hours over the past month, and he couldn't wait to finally talk to her in person.

He spotted Kayla coming up the front steps of the community center.

"Whoa. Look at you," Kayla said.

"What?" He stopped.

"You have a spring in your step. What's going on?"

He shrugged. "I don't know what you're talking about."

She raised a brow. "Are you on your way to pick up

a certain blonde that we've all been missing? Some of us more than others, if the look on your face means anything."

He hadn't realized his feelings were so obvious. "Yes. Now you'd better get inside. You're late, and they're about ready to work on one of your scenes." He tried to be stern, but it was impossible today. He was in too good a mood, even if Kayla had been frequently late to rehearsals recently. He looked at her closely for the first time. "Are you sick? You look a little pale."

"I'm not sick." She looked toward the building. "Like you said, I'd better get in there."

"See you tomorrow." It was good she wasn't sick, but something still seemed off with her. He didn't have time to talk though, if he was going to be there when Estelle landed.

She nodded.

He double-timed it to his pickup. The drive to the airport seemed to take forever, but he finally pulled into the parking garage then headed inside. He checked the departure and arrival board and noted Estelle's plane had landed five minutes ago. They were early. His pulse thrummed wildly. What if he had missed her?

He spotted a short, blonde woman heading down the escalator to baggage claim. Could it be her? "Estelle," he called out, but the woman didn't respond.

Now what? Wait where the flood of passengers exited on their way to baggage claim, or head down a level and meet up with her at the baggage carousels?

Baggage. He pivoted to move with the sea of bodies passing him. Even if she hadn't gone through here yet, he wouldn't miss her downstairs.

"Blake?"

He turned at the sound of Estelle's voice. Relief washed over him. "Hey there, I thought I'd missed you. Welcome back."

She looked good in a pair of white capris and a red sleeveless top. He drew her into a hug. Holding her felt as natural as breathing, but he released her quickly, afraid she'd pull away if he held her too long.

"Thanks." She looked past him. "I thought Amber was coming for me."

"I offered. I hope it's okay."

"Of course. I'm glad you came. I know we talked practically everyday, but I've missed you."

Her words warmed him, and lightheartedness filled him. "I've missed you too."

She grabbed his hand and pulled him along beside her. "Let's go. I need to get my luggage before it walks away with someone else."

He matched her stride, noticing she kept her hand firmly in his. A smile tugged at his lips. "How was your flight?"

"Uneventful. I read two magazines and took a catnap."

"Sounds like a nice trip."

"It was." She released his hand then stepped onto the escalator and rode silently to the bottom level.

People waited in strategic points around the carousel. He and Estelle joined the ever-increasing crowd.

"How was rehearsal today?" Estelle stayed close to him but kept her attention focused on where the bags would come out.

"Good. When I left, Amber was running though a dance number with the kids. They were doing fantastic. I couldn't be more pleased. But you already know that, since I brag on them often."

She shrugged. "I don't mind."

"Good. I blame you for their success."

Her brow furrowed. "Why's that?"

"Your idea to film rehearsals was brilliant. They worked hard to impress you each week, and now they've surpassed where I expected them to be at this point in the summer."

A soft smile touched her lips. "That makes me happy. I'm sorry I didn't call for the past couple of days. I've been busy making sure my new manager felt comfortable and understood my expectations."

"Are you happy with him?" He'd talked to the guy on the phone once and he seemed like a stand-up person. Hopefully things would run smoothly under his management.

"I am. I think he's what the staff needed. He runs a tight ship, but they appear to respect him and want to do their best."

"That's great. I want to hear more on the drive home."

"Home." She smiled. "I like the sound of that."

He studied her face. She looked happy, unlike how she was when she'd left four weeks ago. Funny—he'd expected her to come back travel weary and stressed since she had left her restaurant in the hands of someone new.

Twenty minutes later they were traveling along I-205. He glanced her direction. "I'd love to hear all about your past few weeks. I know we talked everyday, but I'm sure there's lots you left out."

She nodded. "True. I don't know where to start."

"You never said how you figured out your old manager was skimming from the till." He'd been meaning to ask her about it for weeks, but their conversations had been fast-paced and never long enough.

"I had some added security measures put into place. Which included video cameras that only I knew about. I focused them on the two registers. Everyone had to count the till with a witness before starting their shift and then after to make sure it balanced with the receipts."

"Then how did you catch the person, if you made it impossible for them to steal from you?"

"Oh, I left out the important part. The video feed caught the person when they snuck over to the register and took a twenty-dollar bill. At the end of that person's shift, the till didn't balance. I pulled the video and saw who messed with it."

"Very clever."

"Thanks. It helped that no one but me knew about

the new cameras."

"Will you miss cooking?" She'd had to run the kitchen after Jeff left and seemed to really enjoy it. Most of their conversations had included the antics of the cooking staff.

"Yes, but working with the kids here is more fun." She shifted to face him. "I heard from Jeff."

"Oh?" He raised a brow. Unease filled him. "The two of you are on speaking terms now?" He'd carefully avoided bringing up her ex-boyfriend whenever they'd talked.

"Yes. We had a good conversation. I apologized for being an idiot, and he forgave me. I think we both learned a valuable lesson."

"What's that?"

"Both people in a relationship need to have the same expectations of where they want to go as a couple. I enjoyed our time together, but I never saw us getting married. I liked the convenience and security of having Jeff as my boyfriend, but I didn't stop to think about what I was doing to him. I think we both learned that whomever we date in the future, we need to be clear up front about where we're at."

This was the opening he'd hoped for. His palms began to sweat. "With that in mind, if I said I'd like to date you, what would you say?" His hands tightened on the steering wheel. Her next words could make or break where his heart was headed. He was almost afraid to hear her answer, but he had to know before he made a fool of himself.

11

Other than the sound of his tires on the roadway, silence filled the cab of Blake's pickup. From her silence, he could tell his question had taken Estelle by surprise. Did she not see them going in that direction? Should he apologize? Panic seized him. Had their phone conversations not meant as much to her as they had to him?

"Are you asking me out?" she asked with surprise in her voice.

"I am." He shot a quick look in her direction. A little smile touched her lips at the same time her brows furrowed. The smile, though small, encouraged him. "We could get dinner and a movie or go on a hike some Saturday and a picnic, or—"

"Yes."

He chuckled nervously. "Yes to what?"

"A date." She grinned wide now. "But no movies— I've seen everything I want to see, at least for now."

"For real?" He began to relax and loosened his grip

on the steering wheel.

"It's kind of a hobby of mine. I have a movie producer friend who has an in-home theater. You may have heard of her, Alexis Trudeau. She hosts small groups each week."

"Wait—you have a movie producer friend, yet you don't have any offers for movie roles?"

Estelle shrugged. "She knows how I feel. But that's beside the point. I make it my mission to see all the new releases I have any interest in. I suppose I could watch one again, if there's something you really want to see, but it'd be more fun to do something together where we can talk."

He liked the way she thought, but he couldn't get past this new insight. "So you're a movie buff. I had no idea." He would have loved to hear about the movies she'd been seeing over the past weeks. He'd have to pay more attention to new releases and ask before she had a chance to see one. "Now back to the part where you said yes. What are you saying yes to?"

"Yes, I'm interested in dating you to see where things go. But for the record, I'm a wimp in nature." She shivered. "I don't like bugs or dirt."

He chuckled. "Noted. No bugs."

She faced him. "Where do you see yourself in five years, Blake?"

"Uh . . . I haven't thought about it."

"Well, you can't live in Helen's cottage forever. Now that you're dating again, don't you think you should find a real job and a place of your own?"

"Excuse me?" Irritation surged through him. Where did she get off judging him simply because he'd shown an interest in dating her? Derek had warned him about her. He should have listened. He wanted to tell her that where he lived and worked was none of her business, but he held back because he saw her point—even if he didn't appreciate it. "If things are going to work between us, you need to accept me for who I am and not try to change me."

"I wasn't trying to change you. I only asked because I've decided to only date a man I can see myself marrying one day."

His heart hammered. *She can see herself marrying me?* Maybe he'd overreacted. "I'm not sure I like your new approach to dating." He chuckled nervously. "It's kind of a lot of pressure."

She brushed at her leg. "Just keeping it real. I'm sorry for offending you. I can see that I did. But like I said, I don't want to lead a guy on that I don't see myself one day marrying. So if I'm going to date you, I need to know what your future holds. I'm not living in a barn or a studio cottage for the rest of my life."

He held back a laugh. When spoken out loud, his living situation did sound unorthodox. He shook his head. "I understand your point, but what you want is impossible. No one knows the future. We can plan, set goals, and strive for what we want, but there are no guarantees in life. If anyone knows that, it's me." His fingers began to hurt. He loosened his stranglehold on the steering wheel. "It only takes a small decision to alter the future. For example, if I'd agreed to drive my wife and daughter that day, they might still be here, and we wouldn't be having this conversation. Trinity had a tendency to drive too fast, and she was running late because of me. I should've driven them." He glanced her way.

Estelle dipped her chin. "I see your point, but you're wrong about one thing."

He frowned "What's that?"

Her voice softened. "Based on your own theory, you don't know what would've happened if you'd driven them that day. You might be dead too."

He ground his teeth and shook his head. "No way. The chances of that happening are almost nil."

She blew out a breath and waved a hand. "Look, Blake. I'm not interested in debating with you. Their deaths are not on you. You did *not* cause that accident."

"But maybe I could have prevented it." His gut tightened.

She sighed. "Why are you so determined to hang onto the guilt and blame?" Her voice was tender. "It won't change anything. Would your family want you to carry this burden for a lifetime?"

He knew the answer without giving it a thought. There was no way Trinity or Kendal would want that. He'd been carrying the burden of their deaths around for so long, he wasn't sure how to let go. It was a part of him—clearly not a healthy part.

"I'm not one to preach, but are you familiar with the saying 'let go, and let God'?"

"Yes. But I don't see how that applies in my case. I'm not ignoring God's will and doing my own thing."

She reached out and caressed his shoulder. "Aren't you?" she asked softly. "Jesus said in Matthew 11:30 'For my yoke is easy and my burden is light.' He doesn't want you to carry the burden of blame. Let Him have it."

Though her words were spoken with care he was irked and didn't appreciate the Bible lesson. "I didn't know you understood the Bible so well."

"Helen has been a great teacher. Plus I attend church and listen to what is taught."

What was he doing? Estelle would never have said any of that if she didn't care. The fight left him. "I hear what you're saying, and believe it or not, I know in my head you are right, but I don't know how to let go." He wanted to be free from the guilt. His wife and daughter had deserved more. If he didn't take responsibility for not protecting them, what kind of husband and father did that make him? Either way, he'd failed. Of course, Estelle also knew about failure. "You've had some tough stuff to deal with. How did you let go?"

"I've learned to accept that life happens. Don't think I'm being flippant. I feel bad about things I've said and done all the time." She bit her lip. "There are people I've hurt in my past, and sometimes that guilt sneaks up on me. I don't believe I'm supposed to hold onto that guilt though, so I do my best to let it go by picking myself up and trudging forward, because the alternative is worse."

His gut churned. "What's the alternative?"

"Playing the blame game, not living, hiding from life, missing out on the good stuff . . . take your pick. I'm speaking from experience, so don't tell me I'm wrong."

"Yeah, but nothing you ever did caused two people to die." His hands tightened on the steering wheel. "I don't want to talk about this anymore."

"Okay. But until you're ready to let go of the past, I think it would be best if we didn't date after all."

"You're serious?" He glanced in her direction and read sorrow on her face. Talk about a disaster. He should've let Amber pick up Estelle.

~

Estelle stared at the countryside as they zoomed along I-5 near Brooks. Tears of frustration and regret burned behind her eyelids. Hurting Blake was not what she wanted yet that was exactly what she'd done.

"I thought I could ignore that you blame yourself," she said. "That it wouldn't matter. I see now I was wrong. I'm sorry you went through that, and even if we aren't dating, I'm here for you." She should apologize for how harsh her words earlier had sounded, but she wasn't really sorry for anything she'd said. He did need to let go of the guilt he carried, especially since it wasn't his fault.

And she seriously wanted to know his goals and dreams for life. Surely he didn't plan to be a handyman forever. Then again, maybe that's all he wanted out of life. But he had so much more to offer as a screenwriter or playwright.

"After my wife and daughter were killed, I was in a bad way," he said, regret strangling his voice. "Depression and anger consumed me."

She focused her attention on him. Maybe she'd gotten through to him after all. Hope surged through her.

"I hit bottom. Derek came for a surprise visit and found me in a sad state. After that he wouldn't leave me alone. He pestered me every day to move to the cottage on his mom's property in Oak Knoll. Helen's health had improved dramatically, and she was self-sufficient, but Derek wasn't comfortable with her living out in the country alone. He finally wore me down."

"I don't think Derek expects you to keep an eye on his mother for the rest of her life," Estelle said softly.

"Probably not. But we keep each other company."

"She's not *that* old. She could find a man and remarry someday. What ever happened with Nick?"

A tiny smile tugged at his lips. "Remember the day he said to tell her hi? Well, I did, and she decided she needed to run errands in town the next day. She came home with a bag from Deli on the Rye."

Estelle chuckled. "Sounds like a match in the making." Relief soared through her—at least Blake was still talking to her like he used to. A few minutes ago, she was afraid he wouldn't. "So if she and Nick get together one day, what would you do?"

"I'd move. It's not like I'm destitute. I could easily buy my own place." He sent her a sideways glance.

"Good to know. There's something I should tell you. Probably should've told you from the start of this conversation."

"What?" His gaze looked wary.

"Remember my producer friend I told you about?"

He nodded, eyes fixed back on the road.

"I showed her your musical. She loved it. She'll be contacting you soon about optioning it for a made-for-TV movie."

"A movie? But I write plays and musicals."

"It's not difficult to adapt." She frowned. "Aren't you excited? I thought you'd be thrilled."

His mouth opened and closed a couple of times, but he didn't say anything.

Disappointment flowed through her. She'd been so elated to see Blake at the airport and thought for sure his being there was a God thing. Now she wished she'd kept her mouth shut about everything and never pitched his musical to Alexis.

"I guess I'm stunned," Blake said. "I didn't expect you to show my work around. In fact, I figured you'd keep it quiet since you didn't want anyone to find out about your involvement. Thank you for showing her."

That's it? She scratched her head. She sure wasn't in

Hollywood anymore. "You're welcome, but I thought you'd be excited or something."

"I am excited, but it's a lot to take in. I never expected in a million years someone would want to adapt my musical into a TV movie. This is too cool."

"I guess I understand that. I did drop that out of nowhere on you." And she'd enjoyed every minute in spite of his lack of enthusiasm at first.

They passed the sign welcoming them to Oak Knoll. "Why are we in town?" she asked. "I thought we'd go straight home."

"I need to stop by the community center first."

"Will you be a while? I could head over to the grocery store."

"I'll take you there when I'm finished. I'll only be about twenty minutes."

"Then I'll head over to Java World. I want to thank Gabby for sending Cerise my way."

He parked and his eyes held hers for a moment. "Meet back here in twenty minutes."

Her insides leapt at the look in his eyes. She couldn't quite decipher what it meant, but it was definitely a good thing. "Will do." She hopped out then darted across the street. A minute later she pushed through the door of Java World. Cool air whooshed over her, carrying with it the rich scent of coffee.

"You're back." Gabby smiled wide, looking past the other customers in line and focusing on Estelle.

Her face heated as nearly everyone turned and

stared at her. She raised a hand and waved.

Gabby motioned to one of her employees to take over the register. Then she brought someone out from the kitchen to help her make drinks. The line moved pretty fast, but before Estelle got to the front, the shop owner appeared by her side, holding a grande iced green tea.

Gabby thrust the drink toward her. "I made your regular. On the house."

"How nice. Thank you. What's the occasion?"

"You hired my cousin. I could hug you, but I read somewhere that you're not a hugger."

Estelle chuckled. The tabloids never ceased to surprise her with the things they printed. How had they concluded she wasn't a hugger? "You can't believe everything you read." She opened her arms and gave the woman a hug, then stepped back. "Thank you for sending Cerise my way. I don't know what I would have done without her. The staff loves her and my customers love her new menu. Would you care to join me for a few minutes?"

"Sure. We missed you around here." Gabby led the way to Estelle's usual spot, which happened to be vacant.

Estelle liked sitting at the bar because it looked out onto the sidewalk. "Thanks."

"How is Cerise doing? I know you said everyone loves her, but is she adjusting okay?"

"I believe so. When I left, she seemed happy."

"Yes!" Gabby did a fist pump. "I knew she was

perfect for the job. She'd been on the lookout for something new for about a year. But she's so picky about where she'll work."

"I asked her about that." She'd been very pleased with Cerise's answer too. It added to her confidence that she'd hired the right chef. "I really only stopped in to say thanks for sending your cousin my way. I like her a lot, and I think she's going to be great for the business."

Pride shone in Gabby's eyes. "Cerise and I are technically cousins, but she feels more like a sister. My parents took her in when her parents could no longer care for her."

Estelle's heart hurt for the child Cerise once was. "How sad about her parents. I'm sure that was really hard for her. She's an only child?"

Gabby nodded. "So am I. We filled our summers with baking and creating new dishes to surprise my parents each night when they returned home from work. Those were such fun times." She sobered. "I tried to help Cerise forget about her loser parents." She shrugged. "The cooking and baking helped."

Estelle wanted to know more, but the clock edged close to her rendezvous time with Blake. "I think your cousin is happy."

"Good." Gabby stood. "Thanks again. I won't forget what you did for her." Sincerity filled her face.

Estelle squeezed her hand. "Let me know if she needs anything but doesn't want to ask."

Gabby chuckled. "You figured Cerise out fast. She

won't complain. She'll make do. But I'll quiz her from time to time and let you know."

"I appreciate that." She slid off the stool. "I'll catch you later."

Gabby walked her to the door. "Don't be a stranger."

"I won't. See you." She turned and strolled back toward the community center. This town hadn't changed much in the weeks she'd been gone. The flower boxes seemed a little fuller, but otherwise everything moved along as it always did. The warmth of familiarity wrapped around her like the crust on a hot apple dumpling.

She waited for a break in traffic then crossed the street to where Blake's pickup was parked. She looked inside—no Blake yet. Though tempted to go looking for him, she opted to wait. It would be too easy to miss him if he went out a different door. She waited in the shade of his vehicle, resting a hip against the passenger side and pulled out her cell phone.

The click of a camera grabbed her attention. She looked up, shielding her eyes and spotted Mr. Paparazzo. "What are you doing here?" Her pulse surged. Was he alone again or had he brought reinforcements this time?

"Your restaurant fiasco generated some new interest in you."

She looked around. *Lord, please give me courage.* "You're the only one here. Apparently I'm not as big as all that."

"We'll see. Rumor has it you've returned to acting."

He chortled. "In a children's theater. I knew that had to be gossip to throw me off the scent of the real story, so I've been following you."

A shudder ran through her. He'd been stalking her? She knew better than to respond with any expression. That was what he wanted—to capture her with an angry or odd look on her face. The man was excellent at bagging headlines. "I could report you to the police for stalking."

"I can't stalk you. You're a celebrity, so it doesn't count."

"That is one of the most ridiculous things anyone has ever said to me. And I'm not a celebrity anymore. But based on your own words of defense, if you were arrested and your case went to trial, you'd lose. Is this story really worth the risk?"

A hard look covered his face. He lowered the camera.

She raised her chin and narrowed her eyes. She heard footsteps approaching and glanced toward the community center. *Blake.* Relief surged through her.

"You ready to go?" Blake strode toward her, frowning. The pickup's locks clicked. "Is he bugging you?"

She looked to the man who still seemed to be contemplating her words.

"No. I'm leaving. You won't be seeing me around here again, Ms. Rogers."

"Good." She whirled around and opened the door.

Once inside the safety of the pickup, she tried to still her trembling hands.

Blake slid in beside her. "You're not okay, are you?"

She shook her head. "I will be, though. Can we go please?"

He started the engine. "What about the grocery store?"

She sighed. "Skip it. I could stand to lose a few pounds anyway."

"No you can't. I'll stop. Text me your list."

She slid him a sideways glance. His thoughtfulness was like a healing balm. Warmth replaced the prickles of cold the confrontation had caused. She created a short list then sent it to his phone.

His cell chimed indicating her text. "What was that paparazzi dude doing hanging around in town again? He already got his story."

"He wanted more. But I took care of him. I don't think he'll be back, but if you see him lurking around let me know." She was serious about turning the man in to the police.

Blake pulled into the grocery store lot, parked and hopped out. "I'll go fast."

She nodded, then pulled out her cell and called Kayla. "Hey it's me. I'm back."

"And not a day too soon." Strain filled her friend's voice.

Alarm shot through Estelle. "What's wrong?"

12

Blake rushed across the parking lot to his pickup. Estelle wasn't herself after seeing that paparazzi guy. He hated leaving her alone, but at the same time, she clearly wasn't up to shopping. Derek had warned him about her fear of the paparazzi. He had doubted what his buddy told him until now.

He put the groceries in the bed of the truck then climbed into the cab.

Estelle's face was pale, and she looked like she might be sick. Was there something going around? Kayla had the same look about her the last several times he'd seen her. "Are you feeling okay?"

"I'm fine. Just had a shock."

He noticed she had a white-knuckle clutch on her phone. "Did you get some bad news? Is everything okay with your restaurant?" He started the engine to head toward home.

"It's Kayla."

Alarm shot through him. Had his fear for her health

been justified? He'd thought he was imagining things and had tried to ignore the warning in his gut when he last saw her. "What's wrong?"

Silence.

"You're killing me. Maybe I should call her myself."

"No, don't."

"Then what's going on?" This woman could drive a man crazy. Ever since he'd picked her up from the airport, he had experienced a roller coaster of feelings.

"I shouldn't say."

"But you told me it's Kayla so . . ."

She let out a huff. "Fine. But this stops here. Okay?"

He nodded. Fear gripped him, and he braced for the worst. Maybe he didn't want to know after all. No, whatever it was, Derek and Kayla were his best friends. He wanted to know—but why did Estelle know while he didn't?

"Kayla is pregnant and is having horrible morning sickness. She's not sure she can continue with the musical."

He blew out a long breath. "Praise the Lord. I was afraid she was seriously ill." He loosened his grip on the steering wheel. "She hasn't looked well lately. I guess that explains it." He chuckled. "What a relief. I was afraid she had cancer or something horrible."

"Whoa. Now I'm glad I told you. This pregnancy has been rough. She asked me to step in for her. She doesn't think she can continue with the musical."

Confusion filled him. "But doesn't morning sickness pass after the first trimester?"

"I don't know. I've never been pregnant. But even if it does, she'd still be in the first trimester."

"I see. Well, it looks like you've been promoted. How do you feel about that?"

"To be honest, this has been an overwhelming day. I need time to process." She leaned back against the seat and stared at the ceiling.

"Understandable." He could use some processing time himself after the bombshells she'd dropped on him—first about the Hollywood producer and then about Kayla. "Maybe you and Kayla can work something out so she still does one performance. As hard as she's worked, she deserves to do at least one, but she'd need to come to rehearsals now and then for that to work."

"That's a great idea. Let's talk to her about it. But not today. I'm beat."

"Me too." They finished the drive in silence. He parked in front of the barn.

Estelle got out and gently closed the door. "Thanks for coming to get me."

"You're welcome." He'd never seen her like this, and it concerned him. Then again, the drive home had been an emotional roller coaster, plus she had come face-to-face with the paparazzi guy, so it made sense she'd be worn out. "I'll help you with your bags."

"That's okay." She threaded the grocery bag on her arm, wrapped her purse across her body then gripped

157

one suitcase in each hand. "I've got it."

"Okay, if you're sure." He wanted to help her, but if she didn't want it, there was nothing he could do.

"I am. I'll see you tomorrow." She trudged across the driveway and stopped at the path that led to the cottage.

He waited, certain she'd need help. She picked up a suitcase in each hand and stepped from stone to stone. He shook his head and headed for the barn. Thankfully, he had nothing else on his agenda, because all he wanted was to collapse. He went straight to his room and spread out face down on the bed.

Estelle's words from earlier danced around in his mind. What was his five-year plan? She had opened a door for him he'd never considered. If his musical was made into a movie, he would finally make a name for himself. Should he consider getting his own place? If he were honest, staying here long term had never been a consideration. But one day had led to another, and slowly the years had ticked by. Maybe it was time to have a talk with Derek and Helen. Not that he would move simply because of Estelle's comment, but maybe if he moved on, Helen would feel free to follow her heart rather than mother him. He knew she worried about him; and if he was no longer under her roof she'd be free of him.

But before he talked to anyone about anything, he'd pray—something he'd been trying to do more of lately. It seemed Pastor Miller was rubbing off on him.

His phone rang. He checked the caller ID and didn't recognize the number. "Hello."

"Blake Price?" a woman asked.

"That's me."

"My name is Alexis Trudeau. We have a mutual acquaintance."

His pulse amped up. She hadn't wasted any time. He rolled over and sat up. "Right. Estelle mentioned you to me a little while ago."

"Good." She explained her vision for his musical. "My hope is to have this in production by the spring of next year."

His brow furrowed. "Isn't that ambitious?"

"Yes, but I already have interest in the project. Estelle's timing couldn't be more perfect. If you're onboard, I'll go ahead and send you the contract."

He blew out a soft breath. "I'm very interested. Please send the contract." He gave her his email, and they wrapped up their conversation.

He paced to the window that faced the field along the driveway. "Did that really happen?" He couldn't believe it. Estelle had done it. He let out a whoop and ran out of the barn, across the yard, around the house, and through the courtyard. He stopped at the cottage, raised a fist and knocked loudly.

The door flew open. "What's wrong?" Estelle's eyes were wide.

He laughed, and wrapped his arms around her, then twirled her in a circle. "Everything is great, thanks to you." He suddenly realized she wasn't laughing and rejoicing with him. He set her down.

She smoothed her shirt. "Thanks, and congratulations on whatever you're celebrating," she said. Weariness seemed to cover her entire being.

Concern for her pushed aside his euphoria. "Sorry about that. Are you okay?"

"Just tired."

"Okay. I'll be fast. Your friend is sending me a contract."

Understanding lit her eyes. "That's great. Why didn't you say so before accosting me so I would've known what we were celebrating?" She shot him a weary smile.

He chuckled. "Sorry. I don't normally act like a raving lunatic."

"True." She leaned against the doorframe. "Now what?"

He tilted his head and looked down. "Now I slink back to my humble room and hope you'll forget this ever happened?"

"If that's what you want." She raised a shoulder. "Or you could come in, and we can celebrate together while I keep both feet firmly planted on the floor."

He nodded. "I'd like that. I thought for a minute you might be angry with me."

She sighed. "I'm beat. I've been up since yesterday and I—"

"Wait. You haven't slept since yesterday?" No wonder she was so emotional.

"I worked with Cerise last night. I was too wired to fall asleep and had to be at the airport early this morning."

"Okay. I didn't know. We can celebrate another time. I'll leave you alone to rest."

"Sure. That sounds good." She moved to close the door.

He stopped it with a hand. "I'm glad you're back." He meant those words, in spite of being rejected when he'd asked her out and basically told he wasn't good enough for her.

She looked up at him. "Thanks. Me too."

He turned and walked toward the courtyard garden. Time alone was for the best anyway. He needed to think and pray. He cared so much for Estelle, and if he was honest, she was right. He did need to let go of the past, and he needed to figure out where his life was heading. He didn't blame her for expecting him to get his life in order before she would date him.

~

The following morning Estelle rushed to get ready. She'd overslept after tossing and turning half the night in spite of being exhausted. With one last look in the mirror, she sighed. It would take a professional to make her look fresh and youthful today. She pulled away from the mirror and determined not to give her appearance another thought—not an easy task.

She stopped at the door to the cottage before leaving and took several slow, deep breaths, then let them out slowly. *Please be with me today, Lord and help me to be a blessing to someone.* She'd heard Cerise pray that same prayer her first night on the job and liked it so much she'd adopted it.

Estelle opened the door and strolled into the cool morning. Birds sang their songs and sunshine filtered through the trees casting shadows on the ground as she moved across the walking bridge and through the courtyard.

The back door to the main house opened, and Helen stepped out. "Good morning." She smiled. "Welcome back."

Estelle hustled over to her and gave her a hug. "I'm surprised to see you."

"I'm watching the girls today and needed to get some work done before they get here."

"We have a lot to catch up on," Estelle said. "I need to get moving right now, but we'll talk later."

"Sounds like a plan. Don't forget."

"I won't." Estelle made a mental note to stop by as soon as she got back this afternoon. She wanted to get to the theater before everyone this morning. She strolled around the side of the house and noticed Blake's pickup was already gone. Disappointment shot through her. He'd left without her. Sure, she was planning to go on her own today anyway, but he didn't know that. They had always gone together before she'd left.

Her car sat right where she'd left it. A layer of pollen and dirt covered it—another thing to add to her list of things to do. She got in and headed to town. Though tempted to stop at Java World, she kept going and parked near the community center. She didn't need the extra caffeine this morning.

She got out and looked around for anyone lurking in the shadows. Ever since the paparazzo had admitted to following her, she'd been a little creeped out. No one loitered around. Tension eased from her, and she hustled inside. The sooner she got to the stage, the better. She wanted to run through her lines on stage before anyone arrived.

She headed directly to the auditorium and paused at the door still shrouded in darkness. Blake wasn't here?

~

Blake waited outside the church in the crisp morning air for Derek. He couldn't wait to tell his friend about the contract offer.

Derek pulled into the lot and parked. He stepped out of his pickup carrying two cups with the Java World logo. "Hey, man. I thought we might need something hot this morning. It's a little cool for the end of July."

Blake took one of the cups. "Good idea. What is it?"

"Coffee." Derek pulled a sugar packet and two creamers from his pocket and dropped them in Blake's hand.

"Thanks." Blake waited for his buddy to unlock the building then followed him inside to a corner of the foyer where a seating area welcomed conversation.

"Your text was pretty mysterious. What's going on?" Derek eased into the side chair.

Blake pulled the contract from his back pocket before sitting. "I received a call from Alexis Trudeau last night." He handed Derek the contract.

"Who is Alexis Trudeau?"

"You don't know? I thought you would. She's a movie producer. She wants to make our musical into a made-for-TV movie. That's the contract."

"Wow." Derek whistled. "I assume you read it."

"About ten times. Since you wrote the score, you need to be a part of this too."

"This is incredible. How did she get her hands on it?"

"Estelle."

He chuckled. "Of course. I should've known."

"Aren't you going to read it?" Blake was anxious to get Derek's take on the contract.

"I will, but first tell me what you think."

"I have no idea what to think. I have zero experience with this kind of thing." His leg bounced up and down. He set the coffee down. He was already wired.

"All right. I'll take a look and then have my attorney go over it before we sign anything." He set the contract aside.

"What are you doing?" He'd hoped Derek would look it over immediately. He trusted his friend's opinion since he was in the entertainment business and had probably signed many contracts over the years.

"I thought as long as we were here with no distractions, we could talk. It's been awhile."

Blake stopped himself from groaning. This felt like his birthday when he was a kid and his parents wouldn't let him open up his gifts until evening. "I suppose it has. We've both been busy." Maybe Derek was going to tell him Kayla was pregnant. He couldn't believe they'd kept it quiet this long. With their first pregnancy, they told people right away. "What's been going on? Anything new with you?"

"Nothing much other than Kayla's pregnant."

Blake slapped him on the back. "Congratulations! When's the baby due?"

"March."

He nodded. "That's great. Since I have you here, I wanted to talk to you about something else too. You know I moved here to keep an eye on your mom for you."

Derek nodded.

"She's doing fine now, and I wondered how you'd feel if I found my own place. Not right away," he quickly added.

Shock registered on Derek's face. "I didn't see that coming. You do whatever you need to do. I understand needing your own space. I suppose you can't live there forever." He frowned. "But Mom will sure get lonely without someone around the farm."

"Maybe she could move in with you and Kayla."

Derek shook his head. "No. She'd have another stroke with three kids underfoot all the time. I'll figure something out."

He sure didn't want Helen to suffer because of him, but he had faith that Derek would do what was best for his mom. "I'm not in a hurry to move, but I thought I should give you a heads up."

"I appreciate it."

Blake glanced at his watch and rose. "Thanks for meeting me. You'll let me know what your attorney says?"

"As soon as I know something, I'll call." Derek stood and gave him a bro hug.

"Talk to you soon." Blake strode from the building and headed to the theater. It was still early, so he should have the auditorium to himself.

He parked and noted Estelle's car. Odd, she never had her car here. *Oh no.* They carpooled, and he'd left her behind. He rushed inside, swept the auditorium door open. Estelle, rather, Doris the stepmother was on the stage. She didn't break character with his intrusion. He sat in the nearest seat transfixed.

She said her final line then broke character.

He hopped up and clapped. "Bravo."

Estelle screamed. "You startled me."

He strolled toward the stage. "Sorry. You held back in rehearsals."

She shrugged. "I wanted Kayla to shine."

He nodded with sudden clarity. "You are a pretty amazing woman, Estelle Rogers." He leapt onto the stage.

"Don't tell Kayla."

He stepped closer to her. "I wouldn't dream of it."

She looked around the stage, clearly uncomfortable. "What time is it? Do I have time to get some air?"

He nodded. Was she running from him? "Mind if I join you?"

"Don't you have things to do?"

"Nothing that won't keep. I met with Derek this morning."

"Oh?"

He shook his head. "Not here."

"Fine. You can walk with me." She pulled on a lightweight cardigan sweater.

He hopped off the stage then reached up to her. "Come on. I'll help you down."

"I can do it myself." She jogged to stage left and trotted down the stairs.

Disappointment hit him. He'd lost some ground with her, but he hadn't understood how much until now. Stuffing his hands into his pockets, he joined her in the center aisle. "Where to?"

"I could use some herbal tea."

"Java World it is."

They left the community center and strolled side-by-side down Main Street.

"Derek told me about Kayla."

"Okay."

"He's also having his attorney look over the contract from Alexis."

"Good."

These one-word responses were annoying. Had she completely pulled away? He hadn't realized until now how open she'd been with him before. Was he too late?

13

The first of August marked the final two weeks of rehearsal. Estelle sat in the courtyard between the cottage and main house sipping herbal tea. A part of her couldn't wait to head back to California at the end of the month following the performances. Another part wanted to stay in this quaint town forever and take over the children's theater or maybe do an improv night a couple of times a month. A dinner theater could be fun. There was nothing like it within fifty miles of Oak Knoll. She had really enjoyed acting again. She had so many ideas, but no way would she step on Blake's toes. The theater was his brainchild, and it belonged under his direction.

Riding with him to rehearsals every day had become torture, as had rehearsals—a daily reminder of what she wanted but couldn't have. If only he'd let go of the past. She had thought for sure after their talk last month that a seed had been planted and he would change, but she'd seen no evidence. He still carried the burden of blame and seemed set on hiding out on this farm indefinitely.

Sadness settled over her. She missed the connection they'd shared before her trip home. They'd had some fun times. Was she expecting too much from him? Watching him from afar and not engaging in his life for the past two weeks had been agony.

"Good morning." Helen strolled out her back door holding a large mug.

Estelle pulled herself from her thoughts and forced a smile. "What are you up to?"

"I enjoy sitting out here on early summer mornings, listening to the birds."

"Me too. But it's been a while since I've had the time before rehearsals."

Helen settled into the chair across from her at the bistro table. "Have you heard the news?" She placed her mug on the table.

Estelle looked to her friend for a hint about the news and shook her head. "I don't think so." Unease gripped her. Helen looked torn about it whatever it was.

"Blake found his own place and is moving the first of September."

"Really? I had no idea." When had he had time to go house shopping? Rehearsals had been going long and he'd been painting houses nearly every day after. Clearly she was out of the loop, and it was her own fault. Had she been wrong to give him an ultimatum—let go of his past or forget about her?

Helen nodded. "Derek warned me this might happen soon, but I was hoping there would be more time. I'm going to miss having Blake here. Makes me think I should sell and move into town."

"But it's so beautiful on your farm." Estelle couldn't imagine her friend being happy in town. Helen loved her peaceful garden so much.

She looked around. "It is, but it's a lot for one person to care for."

"You've worked so hard to make this what it is."

"It's perfect, isn't it?" A gleam lit Helen's eyes.

"Yes, it is. I'm going to miss it when I'm gone." Helen's farm represented everything she loved about Oak Knoll. Estelle had a lot of fond memories here, from her pillow fight with Blake to her long talks with Helen. This was a special place. She couldn't imagine visiting and not staying here.

"I wish you weren't going back, but I know your life is in California with your restaurant."

Estelle nodded. She wished things could stay the way they were right now—minus what was going on with Blake. Her heart ached from missing the connection they'd once shared. She was so stupid to throw that away. Not for the first time, she wondered if she'd been wrong about Blake's need to let go of the past. Would it be so bad if he didn't? Everyone had at least a little baggage they carried around with them—so his bag was big. She sipped her tea.

"I have a date," Helen blurted.

Estelle set her cup of tea on the table, forcing herself to remain calm and not let her friend know how excited she was for her. "With who?" She allowed a smile to spread across her face.

Helen held her mug between her hands, looking like she might break it in half if her white knuckles meant anything. "Nick. He owns Deli on the Rye. I'm sure you've met him."

"Yes, actually I have. He's a nice man and gave my new chef an excellent recommendation. There's no way I'd forget meeting him. So when's your date?"

"Friday night." Helen's hand fluttered to her neck. "I'm so nervous. The last man I dated was my husband, and he passed away some time ago." She focused on her lap then looked up after a moment. "I feel so out of my element." She met Estelle's eyes. "I need your help. I don't know what to wear, how to act—"

"Okay. It's going to be okay." Estelle used her most soothing tone. "First off, be yourself, because that's who he asked out."

"Right. Good point."

"As far as what to wear; where are you going, and what are you doing?"

"I don't know. He said to dress casual."

"I hate when men do that." Estelle bit down on her bottom lip. Helen wasn't a jeans kind of person, and she'd never seen the woman in a dress. "What about capris and a pretty blouse with sandals? It stays hot until the sun starts to go down, so wearing something cool would be comfortable."

Helen seemed to mull over the idea. "I have several

pairs that would work, but my tops are old."

Estelle smiled. "Sounds like we get to go shopping. I'd love to help you pick something out if you'll let me."

"Of course. There are a few clothing boutiques in town we could check out, or we could go to one of the malls in Salem."

"Let's check in town first. If we can't find what you want, then we'll head to Salem."

Helen's eyes sparkled. "I haven't been clothes shopping in a very long time. I never enjoyed it, but I'm kind of excited now."

She could feel her friend's excitement. "Maybe we can find a new pair of capris and sandals to complete the outfit." Now that she thought about it, Helen's wardrobe was a little tired and out of date.

Helen looked uneasy. "I don't know. I hate to spend money on clothing I don't need."

"It's only one outfit."

"Good point." Her face lit again.

Blake rounded the corner of the house, his brow puckered. "There you are."

Estelle popped up off the chair. "I lost track of time. I'll meet you in the truck. I just need a minute." She headed toward the cottage but spoke over her shoulder to Helen. "Meet me at the community center at noon. We'll get lunch and then go shopping."

"Okay. Break a leg."

Estelle chuckled. The phrase sounded funny coming from Helen. She rushed inside the cottage, deposited her mug in the sink, grabbed her purse, and rushed back to where Blake waited. "Sorry." She lowered her voice. "I have news you're going to want to hear." She two-timed it to his waiting pickup and climbed in. "You started the engine already?"

"I thought you'd be here any minute. When you weren't, I went looking." He pulled forward and drove along the driveway to the main road. "So what's this news?"

"Brace yourself. This is huge."

He only looked annoyed. Seemed someone woke up on the wrong side of the bed today.

If this didn't cheer him up, nothing would. "Nick asked Helen out. They have a date for this Friday. Can you believe it? I can't. I didn't think he had the guts. I mean, sure, it was clear he liked her and all but still—"

Blake's low chuckle silenced her. It grew louder into an all-out laugh.

"What's so funny?"

"You. As excited as you are, you'd think he'd proposed."

She crossed her arms. "Aren't you excited for them? This is a big deal." Had his heart grown so hard that he couldn't even be happy for the older couple?

"Sure it is. But listening to you go on about it was pretty funny."

She rolled her eyes. "Ha ha."

He glanced her way. "Aw come on, don't be like that. I'm only having fun with you. I'm happy for them.

And I'm happy we're talking like this again. I've missed our conversations on the drive to town."

"I suppose we haven't had much to talk about."

"I guess. But this is nice nonetheless."

Warmth moved up her body. He was right. Being together and talking like good friends once again was very nice. But how long would it last? Did she dare hope they'd had a breakthrough?

~

Something was different with Estelle today—something other than her excitement about Helen's date. He slid another glance her way. Her smile radiated over her entire face. She'd been quiet and subdued since returning from California. He liked seeing her like this.

Pleasure bubbled inside him. "It's supposed to be a hot day. You want to get ice cream after rehearsal today?" He asked without thinking, then held his breath, afraid she might reject him yet again.

"That sounds refreshing, but I can't. Helen and I are getting lunch, then shopping for a new outfit for her to wear on her date."

"Oh. Maybe another time." His shoulders sagged a little. He wouldn't ask again. He'd been rejected twice now, and he had no desire to strike out.

Her warm hand rested on his arm. "Hey, I wasn't making an excuse. Helen and I set up our plans this morning. Why not join us for lunch? I'm sure we'll head over to Deli on the Rye. You like it there, right?"

"Yeah. But, I don't want to intrude."

"Are you kidding? Helen would be happy to have you join us, and so would I."

He pulled into a parking space and killed the engine. The sincerity in her voice caused him to turn and face her. He put down the windows. "Before we go inside, there's something I want to say."

"Okay." Her voice softened in uncertainty.

"I've been thinking a lot about the stuff we talked about on the drive back from the airport."

Her eyes widened slightly, but she remained silent.

"I've come to realize that you were right about me needing to get a place of my own. I hadn't given it much thought up to that point, but staying on at Helen's indefinitely was a rut I needed to get out of."

"She told me you bought a place."

It was his turn to be surprised. "You talked about me?"

She nodded and her cheeks lightly pinked.

He rushed on, not wanting to be the cause of a full-out blush, where her face went all blotchy. "I bought a little place on the edge of town. It has a couple of acres with a large workshop. It's actually perfect for me."

"Sounds that way. I wish I could see it, but I heard you won't be moving until after I leave. Congratulations."

"Thanks." Disappointment struck him. He'd hoped she'd changed her mind about leaving Oak Knoll. He'd bought the place with her in mind. He envisioned Estelle cooking in the gourmet kitchen he hoped to add one day. It wouldn't be the same here without her—he wouldn't be the same.

"I think you'd like it," he said. "The yard has an old oak tree that towers over the house keeping it cool during hot days like today."

"It sounds lovely."

"Maybe I can drive you by it sometime." He had known the minute he saw the property it was the one. It needed some work on the inside, a fresh coat of paint, updated fixtures, and flooring, but he'd gotten a great price on the place, so he could afford to freshen the house up.

"I'd like that. Did you know Helen is thinking about selling her place and moving into town?"

His stomach dropped. "Seriously?" If he'd known, he'd have bought her property instead. It was a great piece of land, and the buildings were all in top condition. Helen's place had come to feel like home over the years. He was going to miss it before, but now he'd miss it even more, knowing he couldn't stop in whenever he wanted. "I guess life keeps moving on."

"That's the truth." She paused before opening her door and sliding out. "I'll see you inside."

"Sure. I'll be in soon." He climbed out and locked up, leaving the windows slightly cracked. Even though they were later than he liked, they were still a good thirty minutes early. He strolled toward the town park. *Life keeps moving on.* That's pretty much what Estelle had hammered at him a few weeks ago, and now he saw the truth in those words.

He swallowed the lump that had formed in his throat. Life was going to pass him by while he trudged along carrying a load he wasn't meant to carry. He knew his Bible and what it said. He understood the Lord had healing for him, and it was up to him to receive that healing. It had been five years—it was time to let go.

He found an out-of-the-way park bench and sat in the shade of a lace leaf maple tree. *Lord, you know my heart. You know I feel responsible for Trinity and Kendal's deaths. I know I didn't cause it, and I'm tired, so very tired of carrying this guilt. I give it to you. Please forgive me for hanging onto it.*

You're innocent. The words came out of nowhere.

His throat thickened. He cleared it and blinked away threatening tears. He took a deep breath and let it out slowly. Peace washed over him, and the heaviness lifted. He sat there a few moments longer, absorbing the new feeling, then rose and jogged back to the community center. Cars were pulling up, and kids were getting out and meandering inside.

He stopped as a sudden thought hit him. He was done. This would be his last season as director of the children's theater. He finally felt released . . . free of all that had entangled him. Mrs. Smith would be thrilled. He chuckled then sobered. How would the kids react?

14

"Good afternoon, ladies," Nick said as they strode into his deli. His facial features reminded Estelle of Robert De Niro. No wonder Helen had a thing for him.

"Hi, Nick." Estelle smiled, noting his gaze rested on Helen, who seemed to have lost her voice. She nudged her friend's shoulder and whispered. "Say hello."

"Hello," Helen croaked. She cleared her throat.

"You want your usual?" Nick asked.

"Yes please," Helen said.

"I'll have a green salad with vinaigrette dressing on the side, a fresh fruit bowl, and an iced tea please." Estelle pulled out her wallet and swiped her debit card. "I've got this, Helen."

"I can get my own."

"I know, but I want to treat."

Nick handed her the receipt. "There's a buzz of excitement all over town with talk about the musical. I heard it's being made into a TV movie. I've already bought tickets."

"Tickets?" Estelle asked. "As in more than one?"

"Yep." He winked at Helen.

Estelle winced when her friend's face reddened. She cleared her throat. "We should probably go find a seat." She noted the impatient look on the next customer's face and mouthed *sorry* as they passed.

"I thought Blake was going to join us for lunch?" Helen chose a table near the windows.

"He said something came up." Estelle didn't think much of it at the time, but now wondered what was up. He'd seemed distracted at rehearsal today. More than once he'd called kids by the wrong names—he never did that.

Helen's attention locked onto something beyond Estelle's shoulder. Her face brightened.

"Here you go." Nick placed their food on the table. "Enjoy."

"Thanks," Helen said in a breathy voice.

Estelle ducked her head. This was too much fun. Helen was like a new person ever since Nick asked her out. She couldn't wait to take her friend shopping. She'd noticed on the bulletin board in the community center that there was a concert in the park this Friday night and suspected that was where Nick was planning to take Helen. All summer long the town had held some kind of community event in the park each Friday. This week's concert looked fun—a jazz ensemble from Portland would be performing.

Three hours later, Estelle helped carry Helen's packages into her house. For a woman who didn't enjoy clothes shopping, she'd had a blast splurging on multiple outfits today.

"I feel kind of guilty for buying all of this." Helen held up both hands, each holding a bag.

"I suppose you could return a few things, but you said yourself you haven't bought any new clothes in years. Don't you think it's time to clean out a few things and make room for something new?"

Helen's brow scrunched. "I suppose so. I haven't gone clothes shopping since my husband passed away."

"Sweetie, that's simply too long." How did anyone last that long without something new to wear? Personally she got bored and needed variety. "I know you, and I know you never spend money on yourself. Please don't feel guilty for buying a few new outfits. These are good quality and will last for many years."

Helen's face perked up. "You know what? You're right."

That a girl. "Good." She followed Helen inside and placed the bags beside the door. "Do you mind if I leave these here? I noticed Blake is home, and I want to talk to him."

"Oh? Is there something going on between the two of you?"

Estelle laughed. "You're a doll, my friend. We can't all be as lucky as you when it comes to men." She hugged Helen then went straight to the barn. She slid the large barn door open. "Hello?" she called. "Blake, it's Estelle. Are you here?"

He stepped out of his room. "Hey there. How was lunch and shopping?"

Her insides leapt at the sight of him. There was something different about him, but she couldn't quite place what it was. She stored the thought to ponder later. "We had a great time. Shopping with Helen was like taking a shy child to a toy store. She was hesitant at first, but once she got going, she found several things she couldn't pass up."

He stepped closer. "I'm glad. Derek and I worry about her."

"Well, worry no longer." Her pulse picked up at his closeness. He smelled like sunshine. "I wouldn't say she's cured, but there's an extra spring in her step. Hopefully she won't be so hesitant to treat herself every now and then in the future."

His smile lit his eyes. He grasped her hand, and a tingle zipped up her arm.

"Want to take a walk?" he asked, his eyes pleading with her to say yes.

"Sure." They ambled out of the barn still holding hands. "Where are we walking to?"

"Nowhere in particular." He guided them along the driveway. "Something happened to me this morning that I want to tell you about."

Estelle could barely concentrate on his words with his hand touching hers—talk about a distraction. She pulled her hand from his. "Sorry, I can't concentrate, and I want to hear what you have to say."

A knowing smile tugged at his lips, and she found herself just as distracted as before. Maybe more. "I've made a life-changing decision, and I want you to be the first to know."

Estelle stopped and faced him. Trees shaded the driveway, and a warm breeze rustled the leaves, but it didn't stop the goose bumps from popping up on her arms. "I'm listening." Whatever he had to say, it must be big. Anxiety grew in the pit of her stomach because she sensed his decision was going to affect her too.

"I realized this morning that things were changing. A big part of me was hanging onto the past, and I couldn't move forward until I dealt with the guilt and blame I was holding onto."

She held her breath. Could this be the answer to prayer she'd hoped for? Had she been right after all when she decided to not date him until he let go of the guilt?

"I finally released it, Estelle. This might be something I have to deal with again from time to time, because it's a habit to carry that burden, but I feel free inside." He touched a hand to his chest.

She reached up and placed a palm on each side of his face. "I am so proud of you." She rose up on tiptoe and lightly kissed his lips.

Surprise lit his eyes. "Wow. I hadn't expected that. Thank you, but maybe hold that thought. There's more."

"Okay . . ." Worry niggled her mind. What more could there be? She stepped back and hooked a thumb around her belt loop.

"I also realized I'm done with the children's theater, and I'm ready to pass the reins on to someone with a passion for the arts."

Her pulse thrummed in her ears. She licked her lips. "Do you have someone in mind?"

He nodded. "But I'm not sure if she's available."

Ready to burst with anxiety she blurted, "Who, Blake?"

"I know it's kind of crazy but I thought . . . you."

She let out the breath she'd been holding. "For real?" This was more than she'd dreamed possible.

His eyes locked on hers and held. "You'd be perfect. You have the experience. You already know everyone. The kids love you. The parents love you." He reached out and took her hands in his. "I love you."

Sudden tears pricked at her eyes. "You do?" Love bubbled up inside her. It had been growing all summer, but she hadn't realized it until now.

He nodded.

"I think I love you too. How is that possible, though? We haven't even been on a single date?" She tugged her hands free, placed them at her waist, and stomped a foot. "That's so wrong, Blake. You're supposed to woo me and treat me like a princess."

His eyes crinkled. "Who told you that?"

Jeff had done all that for her, but it wasn't really

what she'd wanted. She'd wanted a friend. A companion. Someone unafraid to accept her challenges and challenge her right back—like Blake did. But she wouldn't let him know that because she still wanted to be wooed now and then. She tilted her head. "That's how they do it in the movies and romance novels."

He chuckled. "We aren't following a script or an outline. Our hearts do what they want. Besides, people don't have to go out on dates and be wooed with gifts and sweet talk to fall in love." He took a step toward her.

Her heart beat a rapid staccato. "True," she said and stepped toward him until they were practically touching, and she could feel his warm breath on her cheek.

"I kind of like our way. Less pressure."

She ran her hands up his chest and looped her arms around his neck. "You make a good point. I don't want to go back to California without you."

"And I don't want you to. As it happens, I've been invited to a certain set that will begin production this coming spring. I've requested a particular actress play the role of Doris, but she hasn't been taking the casting director's calls."

Estelle frowned, remembering several calls she'd let go to voice mail recently. Could it have been this casting director, or was he talking about someone else? She unwound her arms and took several steps back. "Me?"

He nodded with a twinkle in his eye.

"That's what those calls have been about? I didn't recognize the number, so I didn't answer. Why didn't she leave a message?"

"I don't know. Are you interested?"

"Maybe. I thought I'd given up acting, but this musical has given me a fresh perspective. It's been a lot of fun, and doing the movie with you on set would be a blast." She shook her head. "Everything is happening too fast. I need to think. When do they need an answer?"

"Soon. I know they were auditioning a couple other actresses for the part, but it's yours for the taking if you want it."

Her heart pounded. Could she run the children's theater, do the movie, oversee her restaurant, *and* start a new relationship? "I don't know what to say, Blake."

"Say you'll think and pray about it and return the casting director's call."

"I will, I promise."

"Good. Now let's go back to the part about you loving me and me loving you." With one long stride, he closed the distance between them. He pulled her into his arms and kissed her soundly.

She closed her eyes, enjoying every second.

He finally pulled back. "Was that better than the epic kiss at the end of your movie *Tide of Love*?"

She giggled. "A thousand times. But we should rehearse some more anyway."

~

The following day Estelle sat in the park beside Kayla.

Children ran past them playing chase.

Her friend fanned herself with a scrap piece of paper from her purse. "I'm telling you, being pregnant in the summer is horrible."

Estelle shook her head. "But you're barely showing. If I didn't know you were pregnant, I wouldn't be able to tell."

"It doesn't change the fact that my waist is thicker, my ankles are swollen, and I feel uncomfortable in my own skin."

"At least the morning sickness has stopped."

"There is that. Which leads me to why I asked to meet you. I'd like to share the role of Doris with you. I know I gave it to you when I pulled out, but I've been practicing the songs and dances at home, and I won't forgive myself if I pass this up."

"Define share." Estelle and Blake had planned to ask her to take one show, but hadn't gotten to it yet.

"I thought I could do the Saturday matinee." Kayla stopped fanning herself, and looked nervous.

"I think that would work." Relief surged through Estelle—they were on the same page. "I don't want you to have any regrets. I think doing the matinee is a great idea, but you must start coming to rehearsals at least a few times a week. There aren't that many left, and some things have changed since you pulled out."

Kayla's mouth opened slightly. "What do you mean by changed?"

"Don't worry. Come early to rehearsal, and I'll walk

you through everything."

"What if I can't get the changes?" Panic filled Kayla's voice.

"It's not that much. Only a few dance steps and stage placement."

"I didn't realize things would change. I've learned everything wrong." She gripped her hands tightly in her lap.

"Relax. It's not that much, and you'll be able to pick up the new stuff fast. I'll help you. It'll be fine."

"I don't want to make a fool of myself."

"You won't," Estelle said with a firm tone. "Don't you trust me?"

"Of course I do."

"Then know that I wouldn't lie to you. You can do this, Kayla."

Her friend took a breath and let it out in a quick puff. "Okay. I can do this." She shifted on the bench. "You mentioned having something to talk with me about."

"Right. Has Blake talked to Derek in the past twenty-four hours?"

"Not that I know of. Why?"

"Then I have a lot to catch you up on." She told Kayla everything she and Blake had discussed. "Now I have to make some decisions. Do I stay in Oak Knoll and take over the children's theater, do I take the role in the movie, and what do I do with my restaurant?"

Kayla shook her head as if overwhelmed. "You're

forgetting one major thing—you and Blake. When and how did that happen?"

"I don't know. It just did." Her insides warmed thinking about him. She couldn't wait to see him later, but first she had to figure out what she was going to say. She'd prayed last night, but still had no sense of direction.

"That's weird. I don't know how you don't know." Kayla grinned. "But weird or not, I'm happy for both of you. I never thought Blake would find love again."

"I think he felt the same way. I know *I* wasn't looking for it, but I need your help. What do I do about the other stuff?"

She raised a shoulder. "I can't tell you that. What does your heart say?"

"My heart says, I want to be with Blake."

"Where? Here, or in California?"

Estelle paused. It felt right and good here. But California was home too. Why did it have to be one or the other? Couldn't she have both?

15

Friday afternoon Estelle knocked on Helen's door.

Helen opened the door, looking like a disheveled mess. "You're here." She grabbed Estelle's hand and pulled her inside. "I don't know why I ever agreed to this date. I'm too old to date. Look at me, I'm a mess."

"Slow down. You have plenty of time to get ready. Let's go have a cup of tea and talk about what has you so out of sorts." When had *she* become a counselor for her friends? It seemed she was putting out one emotional fire after another this week, and she still didn't have an answer for Blake. Her window of opportunity would close soon. She must make a decision.

Helen nodded. "Tea is a good idea." She turned and rushed to the kitchen.

Estelle hurried after her. Calming her friend down might be more challenging than she'd anticipated.

Helen stood at the sink. Her hands shook, and water spilled off the side of the kettle.

Estelle sidled up beside her. "I'll take care of this.

Why don't you get the tea bags?"

"Okay. Thanks." Helen absently pulled a box from the cupboard and set it on the counter.

Estelle placed the kettle on the stove, turned it on, and then guided Helen to the kitchen table. She sat beside her and grasped her hands in her own. "I'm not very good at this, but I remember you doing it for me a time or two. I'd like to pray for you."

Helen's eyes watered and she nodded. "Thank you."

Estelle bowed her head. "Dear, Lord, my friend needs Your help. She's scared and uncertain. Please be with her. Please give her peace and reassurance that You are always here for her. In Jesus name we ask. Amen."

Helen dabbed at her eyes with a napkin. "I am so proud of the woman you've become. Thank you for praying for me. I feel better already. I don't know why I was freaking out."

"First dates can be kind of scary and nerve wracking, but you both already know and like each other, so you're over one hurdle already." The teakettle whistled, and Estelle stood. "I'll get that." She turned off the burner, grabbed two cups from the cupboard then poured hot water into each one. She should've put the bags in first. Oh well, Helen wasn't the only one out of sorts today. She carried the cups to the table then grabbed the box of tea bags.

They sat in silence waiting for the tea to steep. She needed to give the casting director her answer by five tonight. That was only an hour away. She'd hoped to get some counsel from Helen, but clearly the woman was in no state of mind for that. She'd prayed daily about this and didn't feel clear direction one way or the other. It was almost as if God was giving her the choice to do what she wanted.

Helen touched her hand. Estelle jumped slightly and met her friend's concerned gaze.

"What's the matter?" the older woman asked.

Estelle shrugged. "It's not important."

"Anything that causes that kind of look on your face is important. Now spill. Believe it or not, listening to you, along with this tea, will work wonders on my nerves."

Estelle pulled the teabag from the cup with a spoon then took a slow sip. Hot liquid slid down her throat. "I suppose I should begin from the start. But I'll give you the condensed version since time is of the essence."

Helen nodded encouragingly.

Estelle laid out the facts in less than five minutes.

"Wow." Helen blinked. "That's quite a lot. Since you're clearly rushed for time, regarding your decision about the movie, I have one question. What does your heart say? I believe that when we're seeking the Lord's will, our heart's desire will align with His desires for us."

"Interesting. That's what Kayla asked me."

"My daughter-in-law is a smart woman. She knows the Lord often places His will on our hearts. If you feel no contradiction in your spirit, I'd say follow your heart."

Could that be it then? Estelle wanted to say yes, but

if she said yes, how did she do it all? "I want to do the movie."

Helen slapped the table and beamed a smile. "There you go."

"But what about everything else?"

"One problem at a time. Go make that call. I'll clean up here."

"Are you sure?" She didn't want to bail on her friend.

"Yes. Now scoot. I'm better now. I think I need to take my own advice." She grasped Estelle's hand and gave it a light squeeze.

"Okay, but to be clear, you *are* going on your date with Nick tonight. Right?"

Helen nodded. A twinkle lit her eyes. "Yes, now go. And don't worry about the rest. It will work itself out."

Estelle rushed out the back door toward the cottage, but stopped in the garden. She took a deep breath and let it out slowly to calm her nerves. This was really happening. Excitement filled her, now that she'd finally made a decision.

She pulled out her phone and found the casting director's number in her contacts. "Hi, this is Estelle."

"I've been waiting for your call," the woman said.

"I'll take the part."

"Good. I'll be in touch." She ended the call.

"Wahoo!" She was going to act again. Estelle spread out her arms and whirled around in a circle like she had as a child. When she stopped, the world kept spinning.

She staggered to a nearby bench and sat to catch her breath. She'd never done a television movie before. It would be interesting to see the differences between the big screen and the small screen.

~

Blake paced back and forth in front of the barn. He'd seen Estelle enter the house about thirty minutes ago. He knew she'd been given a deadline of five o'clock to make her decision about the part and assumed she'd sought Helen's advice. What was taking so long?

A loud voice shouted from the direction of the garden. It sounded happy. He froze. *Estelle?* Had she gone out the back door? Of course that was the way she'd go since the cottage was closest that direction. She was clearly thrilled about something.

He couldn't wait for her to come find him. He raced around the side of the house and found her sprawled on a bench, breathing hard. He slowed to a walk and sidled up to where she sat. "Hey there."

Her twinkling eyes met his. She slid over and made room for him beside her. "Looks like we'll be working together awhile longer."

"You took the part?"

She nodded.

Relief filled him. He didn't want to do the movie without her. "Great! You're perfect for the role. No offense to Kayla—she's done a good job catching up.

But you," he wrapped an arm around her, "bring Doris to life."

Estelle rested her head on his shoulder. "Thank you. Next I need to decide about the theater. Before you even mentioned it to me, I wanted to do it, but now that it's an actual possibility, I'm scared."

Shock reverberated through him. "You? What do you have to be afraid of?"

She looped her arm around his bicep. "I've never done anything like that before. What if I can't do it? What if I stink at running the theater?"

"I guarantee you won't stink."

She raised her head and looked at him. "How can you say that?"

"You have good ideas. I also know you won't try to run the entire thing by yourself, which is good, because let me tell you, it's too much for one person."

"Yet you did it for how many years?"

He shrugged. "I was driven, but I think you'll bring some common sense and stability to the theater that's been missing. If you end up forming a board of directors, I'd like to be considered for one of the positions."

"Seriously? I thought you were going to focus on writing."

"I am, but I could spare some time to volunteer for a good cause. Plus how else will I get to see you? You'll be so busy between your restaurant, the theater, and acting."

She raised a brow. "I forgot about Estelle's."

He chuckled. "I don't know how."

"Me neither. But it was only a temporary oversight." She tucked her feet beside her and snuggled against his side. "What do you think I should do? Sell it or keep it? It makes a nice profit, but it's a lot of work when things go wrong."

"True, but doesn't the place pretty much run itself most of the time?" It seemed to him her manager took care of the day-to-day tasks while her accountant took care of the money end. What was left?

"Yes, but I'm ultimately responsible. It helps if I'm there showing an interest in my restaurant. Customers like it and so does the staff." She seemed to be thinking. "I wonder how it would work to live part time here and part time there."

He hadn't thought of that. "What about us?"

"Something else to consider."

He wanted more than anything to ask her to marry him, but she'd basically run from Jeff when he'd proposed. Would she do the same with him? "Can I ask you a personal question?"

"Of course."

He tilted his head. "It wasn't all that long ago that you were in a relationship with Jeff. Are you sure you're ready for another one?"

She smiled seductively. "Are you asking me to go steady?"

"I didn't know you were so old-fashioned. That's

not what I was asking, but I would love to be your one and only."

She sobered. "If you had asked me that question before I left for California, I would have said definitely no, but I've had closure, and I'm much happier now."

Her words didn't surprise him, but he'd needed to hear her say them. "I'm glad. You want to go out on a real date with me tonight? I hear there's a concert in the park."

"I'd love to. Maybe we'll see Nick and Helen there."

"Maybe." Nick confided in him that he'd planned to pack a picnic dinner and take Helen to the concert. It sounded like a good idea to him too. "Would you like to go get some dinner before heading over?"

She looked down at herself. "I'm not dressed for a date. What time does the concert start?"

"Seven."

"Pick me up at six?"

"Sure thing." He stood, drawing her up with him then placed a gentle kiss on her forehead. "See you soon." He turned and strode toward the barn. He had a lot to do in the next hour.

~

Estelle tossed clothes onto the bed, searching for the perfect outfit. Nothing looked right. She should have bought a new outfit when she went shopping with Helen. She plopped down on the edge of the bed with a sigh. What difference did it make? It wasn't like she needed to impress him, since Blake had seen her at her worst. But she wanted to look nice.

Her blue dress caught her eye. Paired with a white sweater and sandals it would be perfect for a summer evening in the park. She quickly changed and freshened her hair and makeup then headed to Helen's house.

Before she could knock, the back door flew open, and Helen stepped out. "I'm so glad to see you. I was hoping you'd head over this way. Do I look okay? Nick will be here any minute."

Estelle took in Helen's small silver hoop earrings, sleeveless, white button-up top, and black capris. "You look lovely."

Relief shone on her friend's face. "Thank you." She paused and seemed to look at Estelle for the first time. "You changed your clothes. Are you going out too?"

"As a matter of fact, I am. With someone you know well."

"Blake." Her face shone with happiness.

Estelle nodded.

"It's about time. I've watched the two of you dance around each other and flirt all summer."

Estelle chuckled. "With the way you're making me blush, I won't need this sweater at all. But you might want one."

"Oh—I didn't think of that. Thanks. Have fun on your date with Blake." Helen headed back inside.

"You too," Estelle called. She strolled toward the

front of the house and spotted Blake as he exited the barn. "Whoa." He wore a black polo style shirt tucked into jeans. How did something so simple look so perfect?

"Hey there, beautiful. I was going to pick you up at your door."

"Sorry." She should've waited for him. Now she looked eager. "I can go back." She raised a brow.

He chuckled. "I imagine you would, but please stay. I'm starving."

"Good to know. Don't get between a man and his stomach."

"Words to live by." He opened the passenger door to his pickup as a black sub-compact car pulled up and parked on the other side. It must be Nick. Too bad she couldn't be a fly on his shoulder when he went to the door. She'd love to witness the couple when they first saw one another. She leaned into Blake and whispered, "Let's try to find a place to sit near Helen and Nick. I want to spy on them."

He laughed. "You're so bad. Don't you think they're nervous enough without us watching their every move?"

She shrugged. "Fine. We can sit close enough to see them but not hear them."

He chuckled and closed the door. A moment later he slid in beside her.

"If they're going to picnic at the concert, why is he so early?"

"I guess they plan to get good seats and eat while

they wait."

"Oh." She should have thought of that. "Where are we going?"

He pointed to a cooler on the seat behind them.

"A picnic?" Excitement bubbled in her. "It's perfect."

"I'm glad you approve. I packed bottled water but thought we could drop by Java World for drinks if you'd like."

"Sure. I'm rather addicted to their peach tea lemonade."

"That sounds good, but I thought you were strictly a green tea person."

"I switch it up from time to time." She sat back and enjoyed the peaceful drive to town. Thirty minutes later, they were seated on a blanket in the grassy park, a discreet distance from Helen and Nick, who'd beaten them there since Estelle and Blake had detoured for beverages. From a distance her friend looked to be having a good time. She still seemed a little shy around her date, but hopefully she'd relax as the evening progressed.

"You're quiet," Blake said.

"Am I? Sorry. I guess I was lost in thought. They're cute together." She nodded toward Helen and Nick.

"Mm-hmm." He looked at her without speaking.

"What?"

"Nothing." He popped a grape into his mouth.

Okay, so maybe she should focus on her date rather

than Helen's. "I'm excited about opening night next week. Are you getting nervous?"

"Not yet."

"I'm glad Kayla will be doing a performance." She had struggled with the new steps at first, but then all of a sudden everything had clicked, and she'd had strong rehearsals since.

"Yeah. She's doing a good job."

Estelle suddenly realized the park had filled up around them, and the concert was about to start. The evening flew by, and two hours later they were home.

They stood outside her cottage door. "Thanks for tonight," Estelle said. "I had fun."

"Does that mean you want to do it again sometime?"

She raised her brows. "Anytime."

He stepped closer to her. "Good." He wrapped an arm around her waist and drew her close then kissed her soundly.

16

The curtain closed, and the audience remained on their feet, cheering and applauding. Estelle grasped the girls' hands on each side of her waiting for the curtain to open one last time. As it swept to the sides, she raised her arms and curtsied deeply. Then she motioned for Jenny to bow. The audience went wild.

Estelle caught Blake's attention and motioned for him to join her on the stage. The audience quieted. She took the microphone from the stand. "Ladies and gentlemen, I would like to introduce to you the creator of *A Week in the Life of Cindy*, Blake Price. Without Blake's inspired writing and Derek Wood's score, this musical would not have been. Let's give them both a hand."

The audience clapped wildly.

"We at the children's theater have some news to share." She looked to Blake, who encouraged her to go on with a nod of his head. They'd argued for an hour about who would break the news to everyone, and she ended up losing by the flip of a coin. "As many of you know, Blake is the founder of the children's theater here in Oak Knoll. He's been running the program with great success for several years. A few weeks ago he asked me to take over the children's theater, and I accepted."

A dull roar erupted in the auditorium. Panic seized her. She looked to Blake.

He raised a hand and took the microphone from her. "I asked Estelle to take over because of her passion and vision for the arts. I have no doubt she will take this program far beyond my wildest imagination."

She mouthed *thank you* to him as the audience began to applaud, a bit more quietly than before.

Blake nodded to someone offstage. Kayla stepped forward and motioned toward the children who all scurried toward her.

What was Kayla doing there, and why was the cast gathering beside her offstage? Kayla's performance had been a smashing hit, but Estelle hadn't expected to see her this evening. She looked to Blake. "What's going on?" she asked, for his ears only.

The audience sat, and a hush fell over them.

Blake put a hand into his trouser pocket then pulled something out. He dropped to one knee in front of Estelle.

She gasped. Her heart beat wildly.

"Estelle, you are a shining star in the night. You helped me live again, and for that I thank you. But more than that you showed me I can love again." He held out

203

a beautiful princess-cut diamond. "I love you with all my heart. Will you marry me?"

She nodded. "Yes."

He rose and wrapped his arms around her. The room was a riot of noise, but she blocked everything out and focused on the only person who mattered. "I love you, Blake, and I can't believe you proposed in front of everyone."

His eyes twinkled. "You liked it?"

"Well . . ." It was in fact her worst nightmare, but she didn't mind as much as she'd imagined she would if ever thrust into this situation.

"Too bad. I wanted everyone to know how much I love you." He dipped his head and found her lips delivering a toe-curling kiss.

~The End~

Author Notes

Dear Reader,

Thank you for joining me on Estelle's journey. She has become one of my favorite characters in this series. In case you were wondering, Oak Knoll, Oregon only exists in my imagination and within the pages of this series. Although real places can be fun to use, and I have done so in other series, I wanted to create my own town for the Melodies of Love Series.

I'm currently writing *A Waltz for Amber*, which I hope to release in the fall. The first chapter is below.

I enjoy hearing from readers and have several ways we can connect. I've put the links below. I hope you join my Facebook Readers Group and subscribe to my newsletter. The Amazon link is for you to be notified whenever one of my books releases.

Finally, if you enjoyed this book, please tell a friend. Word of mouth and writing reviews is the best way you can help me continue to do what I do.

Blessings,
Kimberly Rose Johnson

You may subscribe to my newsletter at
kimberlyrjohnson.com
Amazon follow: http://amzn.to/2jpZj1C
Facebook: www.facebook.com/KimberlyRoseJohnson

Books by
Kimberly Rose Johnson

Melodies of Love
A Love Song for Kayla
An Encore for Estelle
A Waltz for Amber (Coming soon!)

Sunriver Dreams
A Love to Treasure
A Christmas Homecoming
Designing Love

Wildflower B&B Romance Series
Island Refuge
Island Dreams
Island Christmas
Island Hope

Contemporary Inspirational Romance Collection
In Love and War

~ Excerpt ~
# A WALTZ FOR AMBER
Melodies of Love Book Three

1

"Great class today, ladies." Amber Jackson looked to each of her top five dancers in her intermediate ballet class. "Remember we have our first rehearsal for the Christmas recital this coming Monday evening. I need all of you to be here." Without them, the recital would be a flop. "Have a great rest of the weekend."

The girls rushed to the wall where their bags were hung and quickly slipped sweats over their leotards and shrugged into jackets.

Amber loved this time of year, especially in Oak Knoll. The crisp fall air put an extra spring in her step. Humming, *Dance of the Sugarplum Fairy*, she followed after the girls and slid a pair of jeans over her leotard, pulled a chunky black sweater over her head, then drew the pins from her bun and tugged off the band holding her thick hair in a ponytail. She massaged her scalp quickly with her fingers then ran them through her hair. "Much better." She was a bunhead through and through, but wearing her hair down felt really good, too.

"Amber?" a timid voice asked.

Still facing the floor-to-ceiling mirror, she spotted Natalie standing behind her. "Hi." She turned to face the girl. "You did a great job today."

A nervous smile tugged at the teenager's face. "Thanks. But I have some bad news."

Amber's good mood vanished. "What's wrong?"

"I can't be in the recital."

"But you have a solo." The girl practically floated across the floor when she danced.

"I know, but Mr. Daniels scheduled the winter program at school on the same night."

She forced a smile. "We're doing a matinee. Surely you can do both." She'd booked the auditorium at the community center in the afternoon since the rental fee at that time of day was cheaper. Saving money was key as she tried to grow her dance studio and turn a profit.

Natalie shook her head. "No, because he scheduled a dress rehearsal for the afternoon and it's the same time as the ballet recital. If I miss any rehearsals, my grade goes down."

Why was the name Daniels so familiar? "What class does Mr. Daniels teach?"

"Choir. He's new. But he said he graduated from

Oak Knoll High School."

The only Daniels she remembered was a single woman with a young child. She recently started attending the church where Amber's uncle pastored. Her aunt had told her about the woman, presumably since they were close in age, but she didn't remember her from high school. The only other person she knew with that name was someone she didn't care to remember. Thankfully, he'd left town after graduation and hadn't been back since, to her knowledge. She prayed it wasn't him.

"Are you okay?" Natalie tilted her head and touched Amber's arm.

"Yes, sorry. I was trying to place Mr. Daniels, but . . ." She shook her head. "It doesn't matter. I understand your dilemma. I don't want your grade to suffer, so I guess you're excused from the recital." Her stomach knotted. How many other girls would have a conflict thanks to this teacher? Amber had put a non-refundable deposit down on the auditorium.

"Thanks. I'm really sorry. I wanted to do the solo. I love the waltz you choreographed for me."

"Thank you, sweetie." She motioned toward the glass door. "Your friends are waiting."

With a wave, Natalie darted out the door to meet her friends.

"Great. Now what do I do?" She groaned. Natalie was her prize student. She'd hoped the teen would inspire the younger girls. She shouldered her bag and stepped outside the street-level studio then locked up. If she didn't get several more students soon, she would have to close her studio. Maybe moving in with her aunt and uncle like Aunt Merry suggested was a good idea after all. She'd save on rent and be able to apply that money to her business.

She had saved up for years to be able to open her own school of dance. After five months of operation, she'd expected to be turning a profit. She'd been optimistic when several girls from the summer theater had signed up for classes. So optimistic in fact, she hadn't been as careful with her savings as she should have been. Maybe she should create some new fliers and hang them in businesses around town. She strolled along Second Street.

She'd been walking aimlessly and suddenly realized she'd made her way over to Main Street and now stood in front of Java World. Gabby, the owner of the coffee hangout, seemed to know everything about everyone. Maybe she'd have information about this teacher and if she had a chance of changing his mind. At the very least, she'd probably be willing to hang a flier in the window once she made some.

Amber pulled open the glass door and stepped into the cozy shop. The scent of fresh coffee and cinnamon rolls greeted her.

"Good afternoon, Amber," Gabby said. "Long time no see." The thirty-something brunette beamed a smile that reached her brown eyes.

Amber offered a grin she hoped hid the fact

expensive coffee didn't often fit into her budget, but she liked to treat herself every now and then. "Hi there. Could I get a small coffee?"

"Sure thing." She turned and pumped coffee into a paper cup. "I don't think I've seen you in here since this past summer when you came in after rehearsals for the musical. How've you been?"

"Not bad. How about you?"

"Business has been steady. You look a little down. Is there anything I can do to help?"

Amber widened her eyes. How was it that Gabby could read people so well? "To be honest, I'm disappointed and frustrated."

Gabby handed her the coffee. "I'm sorry to hear that. I was going to take a break. Let me grab my tea, and we can talk. Venting my frustrations usually makes me feel better."

She didn't know Gabby all that well so the offer surprised her, but the woman had a reputation for being friendly. "Sure. Talking about it might help." She took her coffee to a corner as far away from everyone else as she could. Not because she was anti-social, but she didn't want anyone to hear her complaining.

Gabby sat across from her with an expectant look on her face.

"One of my best students just told me she can't be in the Christmas recital because her choir teacher won't let her out of rehearsal for the school's winter program." She blinked back tears, surprised at her emotions. "I'm sorry. I know we're talking about a dance recital, but this is so important to me. I put a lot of time and effort into choreographing a dance to feature her strengths." No way would she admit her financial difficulties to Gabby.

Gabby sucked in a breath. "That's too bad. I can understand why you're disappointed. If I could dance, I'd offer to step in, but I have two left feet." She made a sad face. "Can't you work extra with one of the other girls and get her up to the same level?"

Amber shrugged. "I could try, but there's not that much time."

Her face lit. "Sure there is. It's only the end of October. Christmas is two months away."

"True, but the recital is the second weekend in December."

"From what I hear, you're an excellent instructor. I'm sure you could teach that dance to another student." Her eyes gleamed. "Or better yet, you could do it yourself. Your students would love it."

Amber bit her bottom lip and tilted her head to the side. "I don't know. The recital is supposed to showcase the students, not me."

"But you're their teacher."

"I'll think about it." The idea sent her pulse into overdrive. She hadn't performed in a while. Her focus had been on choreography and teaching. She loved to dance, but she'd need to practice a lot to feel comfortable performing again.

The door to the shop opened, and a familiar-looking

man entered. She couldn't place him. Wait, that looked a lot like TJ from high school. What was *he* doing here? Tension knotted her stomach.

Gabby must have noticed her attention had shifted, because she turned and looked at the man, too. "Oh, that's Chris. He started coming in here last month. I think he's new to town."

"Chris? I thought he was someone else. He could be this other guy's twin." Relief washed over her. TJ was not her favorite person, and she'd been happy when he'd left town. "He's cute." She'd thought the same of TJ once upon a time.

Gabby chuckled. "I suppose he is, but he's much too young for me."

"How old *are* you?" Amber pursed her lips after the words popped out. She really needed a stronger filter.

Surprise lit Gabby's eyes. "Let's just say I graduated about ten years before you."

"No way. You look much younger than thirty-seven."

"Thanks." She stood. "Break's over, so I need to get back to work. Don't forget what I said. There's no reason you can't do that dance yourself."

"I won't forget." Funny that Gabby was so strict about her break time since she owned the place. Then again, she probably wanted to hold herself to the same standard as her employees.

Amber studied Chris from behind. He'd been in town over a month, and her not seeing him before now was crazy. Then again, Oak Knoll had grown by several hundred people this past year due to the cost of housing in the surrounding areas. Thankfully, her hometown had managed to escape the housing crisis so many others faced. But if too many more people moved here, it would become a problem.

Chris walked to the other end of the counter and picked up his order. Was he a coffee or tea drinker? He suddenly turned and looked directly at her.

She gasped and looked down. Her face heated. He'd caught her staring. She pulled out her phone and pretended to text someone.

"Excuse me."

She looked up—*Chris*. "Hi."

"The owner said I should come over and say hi."

Amber shot a look toward Gabby. "Really? I wonder why."

A confused expression settled on his handsome face, and he glanced over his shoulder at Gabby. "So you don't need to talk to me?"

She shook her head. "But as long as you're here, you're welcome to join me. Unless you're waiting for someone?" She'd never been shy, but Gabby's boldness took things to a new level, to her way of thinking.

"I'm not." He hesitated. "You're the spitting image of someone I went to high school with. I almost feel I know you."

"I had the same thought when you walked in."

He pulled out the chair Gabby had vacated and sat.

Chris was cuter up close than he had been at a distance. He had a boy-next-door look about him with his dark hair swept to the side of his forehead. "I grew up here, but it's been several years since I've been around. Maybe that's why we seem familiar to each other."

She stilled. "You grew up here?"

He nodded then went on to tell her the year he graduated and about his family without giving her a chance to respond. "My dad was really into sports, so I played football and baseball."

He'd graduated a year ahead of her, and he was a jock. Unease settled in her stomach. "Did you happen to go by the name TJ in high school?"

His face lit. "Yes! T for Tom and J for Junior. I don't care for my first name, and I didn't want to go by TJ as an adult. I go by my middle name now. So you remember me? I wish I could place you. How did we know each other?"

Her pulse galloped out of control. TJ Daniels. She took a calming breath, forcing herself to behave like an adult and not a hurt teenage girl. "We didn't. You were a year ahead of me." And she'd had a huge crush on him until she'd overheard him making fun of her to one of the other guys on the baseball team. "I was a dancer—a bunhead. You might remember me better if my hair was pulled into a bun."

His smile faded. "I remember. You were a ballet dancer."

"Still am. I own Pointe Dance Studio on Second

Street." Did he remember mocking her after the talent show? Wait a minute. She narrowed her eyes. "Weren't you in choir in high school?"

He nodded, still looking uncomfortable. "Yes. I'm the choir teacher at the high school and the middle school now."

She sucked in a sharp breath. This day kept getting worse. She sat up taller. "So you're the person I need to talk to about getting my student excused from rehearsal to perform in my Christmas recital."

He frowned. "You're Natalie's dance teacher?"

"I am. She's incredibly talented and—"

He raised a hand. "I'm sorry, but I can't make an exception for one student. Then everyone will expect the same."

Telling him he was as big a jerk now as he was in high school sat on the tip of her tongue, but "I see" came out instead. Maybe her filter was working better after all. She stood.

"You look angry." His brow furrowed. "It's nothing personal. I have rules in my class, and I have to enforce them. If I didn't, my students wouldn't respect me, and we wouldn't be on track to win a few competitions this year."

She took a calming breath. Her entire body shook. She clenched the seatback. "Congratulations." She raised her chin and marched toward the exit.

A chair scraped against the floor. "Hey, wait."

She stopped and nearly got trampled by him.

He took a step back. "Sorry. I didn't expect you to stop."

"You said to wait." She glared and didn't even care. She tried hard to be nice to everyone, but TJ, or rather Chris, didn't count.

He chuckled and rubbed the back of his neck.

"What do you want?"

"Uh, nothing I guess. Maybe I'll see you around."

"I hope not," She muttered under her breath, nodded, and forced herself to walk, and not rush, the rest of the way to the door. What would she do now? Why did the choir teacher have to be Chris Daniels, of all people? She might have stood a chance with someone else, but not him.